W9-AAY-840

# Mmm. Mail-Order Meat!

I tipped the receiver off the phone and pressed redial. I could hear a ringing sound on the other end and then someone answered, "Fabulous Gormet mail-order. How can I help you?"

Thank goodness for twenty-four-hour service.

"Hello," I whispered. "I placed an order this afternoon, but didn't have my credit card."

"Last name?"

"Chandler."

"Yup, here it is. You've got your credit card now?"

"Yes."

"Could you read the numbers to me?"

In the dim glow of the night-light, I read off the numbers.

"Will we be shipping to the same address as the credit card billing address?"

"Yes," I said.

"Thank you. Your order will go out tomorrow morning. You should have it the following day."

I knew what I'd done was wrong. But I was driven by instinct . . . by survival of the fittest. And if I didn't get that meatloaf soon, I was going to have a fit!

Look for:

*Wordsworth and the . . .*

*Cold Cut Catastrophe*
*Kibble Kidnapping*
*Roast Beef Romance*
*Mail-Order Meatloaf Mess*
*Tasty Treat Trick*°
*Lip-Smacking Licorice Love Affair*°

From HarperPaperbacks

° coming soon

**ATTENTION: ORGANIZATIONS AND CORPORATIONS**

Most HarperPaperbacks are available at special quantity discounts for bulk purchases for sales promotions, premiums, or fund-raising. For information, please call or write:
**Special Markets Department, HarperCollins*Publishers*,**
**10 East 53rd Street, New York, N.Y. 10022.**
**Telephone: (212) 207-7528. Fax: (212) 207-7222.**

# Wordsworth and the Mail-Order Meatloaf Mess

by Todd Strasser

**HarperPaperbacks**
*A Division of HarperCollinsPublishers*

If you purchased this book without a cover, you should be aware that this book is stolen property. It was reported as "unsold and destroyed" to the publisher and neither the author nor the publisher has received any payment for this "stripped book."

This is a work of fiction. The characters, incidents, and dialogues are products of the author's imagination and are not to be construed as real. Any resemblance to actual events or persons, living or dead, is entirely coincidental.

HarperPaperbacks   *A Division of* HarperCollins*Publishers*
10 East 53rd Street, New York, N.Y. 10022

Copyright © 1995 by Todd Strasser
All rights reserved. No part of this book may be used or reproduced in any manner whatsoever without written permission of the publisher, except in the case of brief quotations embodied in critical articles and reviews. For information address HarperCollins*Publishers,*
10 East 53rd Street, New York, N.Y. 10022.

Cover and interior illustrations by Leif Peng
Cover and interior art ©1995 Creative Media Applications, Inc.

First printing: December 1995

Printed in the United States of America

HarperPaperbacks and colophon are trademarks of HarperCollins*Publishers*

❖ 10 9 8 7 6 5 4 3 2 1

*Michael, Christine, and Brian Garvey*

# Wordsworth and the Mail-Order Meatloaf Mess

# One

―――❊❊❊―――

**"Come on, Wordsworth, time for a walk,"** Dee Dee said.

I was in the middle of a wonderful dream. I was the king of all dogs. I sat on a red satin doggie bed atop a golden throne. Before me stretched a long line of my canine subjects. Each one pulled a small cart filled with cold cuts, juicy steaks, and mouth-watering roasts.

"Wordsworth . . ." Dee Dee nudged me on the shoulder.

"Get back in line, peon," I grumbled, still half asleep.

"What line?" Dee Dee asked.

"I'll start with the rib roast," I commanded in my dream.

Dee Dee shook her head wearily. "Dreaming about roast beef again. I should have known."

My eyes opened. I was lying on my back on the kitchen floor. Dee Dee was standing over me with her hands on her hips. Darn! I wanted to go back to my dream!

"Can't you think about anything else?" she asked.

"Uh, veal shank?"

She kneeled down and rubbed my tummy affection-ately. "No, silly, I meant anything *except* food."

"Why?" I asked.

You've probably noticed by now that I can talk. This shouldn't come as a surprise to you. After all, we basset hounds are by far the most intelligent breed of dog. It was only a matter of time until one of us proved it.

"Because there's more to life than food," Dee Dee said.

"Not to *my* life," I said. Well, that wasn't quite true. I am also very fond of Dee Dee. I just don't tell her.

Dee Dee stood up again and crossed her arms. She's ten and my best friend. I live with her family, the Chandlers. But Dee Dee's the only one who knows I can talk.

"Wordsworth, you know I love you," she said. "You know I'd never purposefully say anything to hurt your feelings, but you've gotten fat."

Still lying on my back, I lifted my head and looked down at myself. My sturdy, muscular legs were sticking up in the air.

"I am a large and powerful beast," I said.

"You are a blob," said Dee Dee.

What an insult! I stared up at her, feeling hurt. "Is that any way to treat a friend?"

"It is if the friend really loves and cares about you," Dee Dee said. "If you get any fatter your tummy is going to drag on the ground when you walk."

"Never," I said. To prove it I rolled over and got up. Well, I *tried* to get up. My paws kept slipping on the kitchen floor.

"See? You can't even get up by yourself anymore," Dee Dee said.

"Of course I can. It's the floor. It's too slippery. Someone must have just polished it."

Dee Dee bent down and slid her hands under my legs to help me up. "No one's polished this floor in years. I'm worried about you, Wordsworth. I really am. I think we're going to have to do something."

Uh-oh. She sounded serious.

"Like what?" I asked.

"I'm not sure. A diet, I guess."

I stared up at her in horror. "Don't you think that's a little drastic? I mean, maybe I've gained a few *ounces*, but it's nothing serious. Surely I—"

"Shush!" Dee Dee held up her hand. "Someone's coming."

We heard footsteps clomping down the stairs. Dee Dee pressed her finger to her lips, reminding me not to talk. A moment later Roy, Dee Dee's fourteen-year-old brother, came into the kitchen. Roy has reddish hair and freckles. He spends most of his time lifting weights and watching TV.

"Mail come yet?" he asked.

"Yes, and there was no letter from Razel," Dee Dee said.

"Darn." The corners of Roy's mouth drooped. He

**3**

looked disappointed. Razel was a girl he'd met over the summer. Everyone knew he had a crush on her.

Roy turned to his younger sister. "Dee Dee, if you were a girl—"

"I *am* a girl," Dee Dee said.

"Yeah, but I mean, if you were older. And a boy sent you a letter, wouldn't you write back?"

"I guess." Dee Dee shrugged. "Maybe Razel's busy. Maybe she hasn't had time to write back. How long ago did you send the letter?"

"Two days ago," Roy said.

Dee Dee rolled her eyes in disbelief. "Two days? She probably hasn't even *gotten* the letter yet."

"You think?"

"Roy, it's the fall," Dee Dee said. "We went on a field trip to the post office last week, and they said this is the start of the busiest time of the year."

"You're probably right." Roy looked relieved.

"I'd wait at least a few more days before you decide she really hates your guts," Dee Dee advised him.

"Okay." Roy went to the refrigerator and pulled it open. I quickly joined him and gazed hungrily up at that cold treasure chest of delights. Roy reached in and pulled a drumstick off a roast chicken on a platter.

"*Yip! Yip!*" A hungry whimper rose from my throat.

"Oh, sure, Wordsworth, here you go." Roy tore a thick wedge of breast meat off the chicken and tossed it to me.

I caught it in mid-air and quickly gobbled it down. *Hmmm* . . . It was delicious, juicy, just right.

Dee Dee's eyebrows dipped into an angry V. "Roy!" she said angrily.

"What?" Roy looked surprised.

"Don't feed Wordsworth anymore."

"Why not?"

"Gosh, Roy, look at him."

Roy looked down at me. His eyes widened slightly. "Wow, Wordsworth, you've put on weight."

"If he gets any heavier his tummy is going to drag on the ground," Dee Dee said. "He'll be an embarrassment."

I quickly sucked in my tummy and lifted my head and tail, affecting the regal stature of my forefathers.

"Hey, check it out," Roy said. "Now he looks okay."

"Just wait," Dee Dee said. "Sooner or later he has to take a breath."

She was right. I was holding my breath. As soon as I exhaled, the regal stature of my forefathers sagged in the middle. Keeping a regal stature took too much effort. I laid down on the kitchen floor and yawned.

"Don't get too comfortable, Wordsworth." Dee Dee went to the kitchen closet and got out my leash. "We're going for a walk."

# Two

―――⚬⚬⚬⚬――

**"How come you're so mean to me?"** I grumbled as we walked through Soundview Manor Park near the Chandlers' house. It was a crisp, cold October day. The leaves were red, orange, and yellow and people were wearing coats and hats.

"I don't want to be mean," Dee Dee replied. "I really love you, Wordsworth. I'm just worried about you. It's not healthy to get so fat."

"Don't exaggerate," I said. "I'm not *that* fat. I've simply bulked up. Marathon runners do it all the time."

"But they run marathons," Dee Dee said. "You just sleep."

"Okay, from now on I'll dream about marathons," I said, and stopped to sniff the base of a tree.

"Somehow I don't think that will help you lose weight," Dee Dee said. She tugged gently on my leash. "Please come on, Wordsworth. You can't get any exercise if you stop to sniff every tree."

"But I'm a dog," I said. "I have to sniff things. It's in my genes."

"You sniff the same trees every day," Dee Dee said.

"I have to make sure nothing's changed."

Just then a squirrel hopped from a tree trunk and raced across the ground near us.

"Go, Wordsworth!" Dee Dee cried. "Chase it!"

"Why?" I gave her a puzzled look.

"Because all dogs chase squirrels," she said. "That's also in their genes."

"Not mine," I said. "I've evolved."

Dee Dee rolled her eyes. "You just won't do anything that might mean exercise."

I shivered. Even the *word* exercise gave me chills.

Just then a lightly perfumed scent wafted by in the air. It was clearly from a female of my species, but I didn't recognize it. Had someone new moved into the neighborhood? Curious to see, I started in the direction of the scent.

Dee Dee immediately pulled back. "I'm sorry, Wordsworth. I know you must smell food, but I can't let you have any."

Before I could tell her that it wasn't the scent of food I was following, from around the corner came a very pretty cocker spaniel. She had long light-brown hair just like Lady from *Lady and the Tramp*. And the most adorable big brown eyes.

I immediately sucked in my tummy and raised my

head and tail. She paused and perked up her ears. Except for the fact that she wasn't a basset hound, she was about the cutest canine I'd ever seen.

The boy walking her looked to be about the same age as Dee Dee. He had short black hair and was wearing a hooded sweatshirt. He smiled shyly at us.

"Hi," said Dee Dee, who is anything but shy.

"Uh, hi," said the boy.

"That's a really pretty cocker spaniel," Dee Dee said.

"Thanks," said the boy. "Her name's Nicole."

*Nicole*, I thought. Very French.

"I've never seen you around here before," Dee Dee said.

"We're living over there." He pointed toward the far side of the park. "My name's Zander."

"I'm Dee Dee and this is Wordsworth. We live over there." Dee Dee pointed in the opposite direction from the way Zander had pointed.

Meanwhile, Nicole sat demurely at Zander's feet and watched me. I wanted to say something friendly, but I couldn't because I was working so hard to hold my tummy in. Of course, the only way I could do that was by not breathing.

Not knowing what else to say, Zander said good-bye. He and Nicole walked past us. As they left, Nicole turned and looked back at me with a friendly smile. I felt my heart start to melt. What a doll!

As soon as they were out of sight, I let my tummy

out. The effort of holding it in had exhausted me. I flopped down on the ground, huffing and panting.

Dee Dee smiled knowingly at me. "Well, well."

"What's with you?" I asked as I gasped for breath.

"You like her," Dee Dee said.

"Who?" I pretended not to know.

"Oh, come on, Wordsworth. She's gorgeous."

"You mean, Nicole?"

"Don't pretend you don't know. I saw how you acted when you saw her."

"What are you talking about?" I was still playing dumb.

"You were so self-conscious you couldn't even talk," Dee Dee said. "You just stood there trying to keep your tummy tucked in."

"Did not."

"Did too," Dee Dee said with a grin. "Tell me she isn't cute."

"Oh, she's cute all right, but not my type," I said.

Dee Dee gave me a sly look.

"What's that look supposed to mean?" I asked.

"Don't worry, your secret's safe with me." She winked.

# Three

———— ⟨≋⟩ ————

**Frankly, I think my *secret* was mostly in** Dee Dee's imagination. But it would do no good to try and persuade her that I hadn't fallen madly in love with Nicole. Dee Dee was at that age when girls first start to think about love. It must be like fleas. Once you have it, you can't avoid spreading it to everyone around you.

Anyway, by the time we got back from the walk, I was pooped. It didn't seem like we'd walked any farther or faster than usual, but I was so tired that I could barely drag myself through the gate into the backyard. And forget about climbing up the back steps onto the deck and into the kitchen. I laid down at the bottom of the steps.

"What are you doing?" Dee Dee whispered. Through the sliding glass door we could see her parents sitting in the kitchen. Dee Dee had to make sure they didn't see us talking.

"Taking a nap," I replied with a yawn.

"At the bottom of the steps?"

"Sure," I said. "It's as good a place as any."

Dee Dee pursed her lips and gave me a sad look. "I'm really worried about you, Wordsworth. You don't even have the energy to climb a few steps."

"Just give me a second," I whispered.

"All right," she whispered back. "But I really think we have to do something about you."

A few minutes later, I got to my feet and started up the steps. I climbed the first two by myself, but then began to feel out of breath again. Luckily, Dee Dee got behind me and gave me a push.

We got up to the deck and Dee Dee pulled open the sliding door while I went into the kitchen through my doggie door. Flora and Leyland Chandler were sitting at the kitchen table. They're Dee Dee's parents. The kitchen table itself was covered with piles of paper and envelopes.

I flopped down on the kitchen floor and panted for breath.

Leyland looked up at Dee Dee. He's a tall, thin man with long white hair. "You took Wordsworth for a run?"

"No, we hardly had a walk," Dee Dee said. "He stopped to sniff almost every tree in the park. Then he had to rest before he went up the deck stairs. I even had to help him up."

"Then why is he so out of breath?" Flora asked. She is an elegant woman with long blond hair. She always wears white.

"Gosh, Mom, *look* at him."

Leyland and Flora both stared down at me.

"My, he has gotten rather rotund," Flora said.

"I can't imagine that it's healthy for a dog to put on that much weight," said Leyland.

"It's because we're always giving him scraps at meals," Dee Dee said.

"Oops," cried Flora. Some of her papers slid off the table and onto the floor. I noticed that they had long columns of numbers on them. Dee Dee helped her pick them up.

"Thank you, darling," Flora said. "Now where did I put my reading glasses? I can't see a thing without them."

"Here they are." Dee Dee handed them to her mom. Then she pointed at the pieces of paper. "What are these?"

"These are bills, darling," Flora explained.

"Bills?" Dee Dee frowned.

Just between you and me, I would think that in most households children by the age of ten know what bills are. But the Chandler household isn't like most.

"They're for our credit cards, telephone, heat, and electricity," Flora said.

"Once a month your mother and I sit down and pay them," Leyland added.

"But they're not here," said Dee Dee.

"Who?" asked Flora.

"The people you're paying."

"That's right," said Leyland. "So we write these checks and send them to everyone we owe money to. And we know who we owe money to because they send us these bills."

Just then, Janine came into the kitchen. Janine is Dee Dee's older sister. She is sixteen and has long blond hair and is considered quite beautiful by human standards. She was wearing her field hockey uniform. Her socks were dirty and her cleats had left a trail of mud through the house.

"Hello, darling," Leyland said. "How was your game?"

"Great, Dad." Janine bent down and kissed him on the forehead.

"Several boys called," Flora said, handing Janine a piece of paper. "I took their names and phone numbers."

"Thanks, Mom." Janine crumpled up the paper and dropped it in the garbage can. Then she went to the refrigerator and pulled it open, looking for something cold to drink.

Despite being exhausted from my walk, I somehow managed to drag myself over to the fridge and whimper.

"Don't you dare, Wordsworth," Dee Dee warned me.

I gave her a sad look. Didn't she understand that all that exercise had left me starving?

Dee Dee shook her head as if she knew what I was thinking.

"I'm sorry, but you'll never lose weight if you keep eating," she said.

Darn! I went back to my spot on the floor and laid down again. Meanwhile, Janine took out a container of orange juice and sat down at the kitchen table with her parents.

"Mom, Dad, could I talk to you for a second?" she asked.

Flora and Leyland looked up from their work. "Yes, dear," said Flora, "what is it?"

"I think it's time you let me get a credit card," Janine said. "I'm sixteen years old and now that I have a junior driver's license, I need to put gas in the car. I shop for all my own clothes and I need to pay for stuff when I go out with my friends. If I had a credit card I wouldn't have to worry about having enough money all the time. It would make my life a lot easier."

"What do you think?" Leyland asked Flora.

"She's right," Flora said with a nod.

"Oh, great! Thanks!" Janine hugged both of her parents and kissed them on the cheek. Then she left the kitchen. Mr. and Mrs. Chandler turned back to their bills.

"Mom? Dad?" Dee Dee said.

Her parents looked up. "Yes, dear?"

"Could I have a credit card, too?"

Leyland frowned. "Whatever for, dear?"

"Oh, you know," Dee Dee said, "if I want to buy a toy or some candy."

"We can always give you money for that," said Flora.

"But what if it's something expensive?" Dee Dee asked.

"Like what?" asked Flora.

Dee Dee looked around, as if trying to think of something. Her eyes settled on me. "Like taking Wordsworth to Dr. Hopka."

My ears perked up in fear at the sound of that dreadful man's name.

"He always sends us a bill, dear," Flora said.

"That reminds me," Leyland said, sifting through his papers and picking up a postcard. "This came the other day. It's a notice from Dr. Hopka that it's time for Wordsworth's annual checkup."

*Owwwwwwooooooooooooo!* I sat up and howled in despair.

# Four

**"Wordsworth, get over here right now!"**
Dee Dee demanded.

It was three days later. Dee Dee was holding my leash. I was hiding under the coffee table in the living room.

"No!" I said.

"Wordsworth!" Dee Dee yelled.

"Forget it," I muttered. "I'm not going."

The rest of the Chandlers were out running errands. Dee Dee and I were home alone.

"You have to," Dee Dee insisted.

"Says who?"

"Everyone gets an annual checkup," she said. "Me, Roy, Janine, even Mom and Dad."

"But Dr. Hopka's going to give me a shot."

"You don't know that."

"He *always* gives me shots."

"Maybe he won't this time."

**17**

"Liar."

Dee Dee got down on her hands and knees and gave me a sympathetic look under the table. "Wordsworth, doctors are good for people."

"Maybe they're good for people, but they're not good for dogs."

"Yes, they are. If Dr. Hopka gives you a shot, it's for a good reason. It's so you won't get sick. You have to go."

"No."

The front door opened and Janine and Roy came in. They found Dee Dee on her hands and knees talking to me.

"Don't tell me you're talking to that dog again," Janine groaned.

"Did the mail come?" Roy asked eagerly.

"Yes," Dee Dee said. "Sorry."

Roy's shoulders sagged. "It's been five days. I even sent her a second letter in case the first one got lost in the mail."

"I have letters boys wrote me three years ago that I still haven't answered," Janine said.

"*That's* encouraging," Roy grumbled gloomily.

"Could you guys help me get Wordsworth out from under the coffee table?" Dee Dee asked.

"Why?" asked Janine.

Dee Dee explained how I had an appointment with Dr. Hopka, and that I didn't want to go. Then they started whispering. I knew they were planning something.

• • •

A few minutes later, Janine and Roy spread an old blanket out on the floor near the coffee table. Then Dee Dee came in with a freshly broiled lamb chop on a plate and put it on the middle of the blanket.

"Oh, well," Roy said, "guess I'll go watch some TV."

"I think I'll go with you," said Dee Dee.

"I'm going to do some homework," said Janine.

They all left the room, leaving the blanket and lamb chop behind.

It was such an obvious trap. They *had* to be crazy to think I'd fall for that one!

But the scent of that lamb chop made my mouth start to water.

I fought the urge to eat. There was no way I was going to leave the shelter of the coffee table.

But that tasty meat was so tempting . . .

They were probably waiting in the next room. As soon as I came out, they'd scoop me up in the blanket and drag me to Dr. Hopka's office.

But the longer that lamb chop sat there, the more my stomach grumbled hungrily.

Maybe, if I was really quick, I could rush out, grab the lamb chop, and get back under the table before they caught me.

No, no, that was *just* what they expected me to do!

The smell of that juicy chop was making me delirious.

I had to do it, no matter what the risk.

No! It was suicide!

I didn't care!

I crept out from under the coffee table and pounced!

"He's out!" a voice cried.

In a flash, Roy, Janine, and Dee Dee rushed into the room and grabbed the blanket, pulling up the ends like a sack. I was trapped inside.

But I had that lamb chop.

# Five

~~~~~

**"This has to be the most embarrassing**
thing you've ever done to me," I muttered in the dark.

"Shush, someone will hear you," Dee Dee said as she
pushed me in an old baby carriage toward Dr. Hopka's
office. I was still wrapped in the blanket. Janine had tied
the ends so that I couldn't get out. Then they'd put me
in the carriage so that Dee Dee could push me.

"At least untie the blanket so I can see," I said.

"Not until we're in the office," Dee Dee said. "Otherwise you'll run away."

"I promise I won't," I said. "Don't you believe me?"

"No."

"Some friend you are."

"That's right, Wordsworth," Dee Dee replied. "Only
a friend would care enough about you to do this. How
do you think I feel, pushing a baby carriage with a dog
in a blanket?"

"At least share it," I said.

"Share what?"

"The dog in the blanket," I said, picturing those delicious little hot dogs in batter that they serve at parties.

"No, silly, *you're* the dog in the blanket," Dee Dee said.

"Oh, yeah."

"Uh-oh!" Dee Dee whispered.

"What?"

"You won't believe who's coming toward us."

"Who?"

"Just keep quiet."

A moment later Dee Dee slowed the carriage and I smelled that wonderful delicate scent again. My heart started to flutter. It was Nicole!

"Oh, uh, hi," a boy said.

"Hi, Zander," Dee Dee said. "We met in the park, remember?"

"Oh, yeah, so where's your dog?"

"Wordsworth's at home. How's Nicole?"

"I think she's a little lonely," Zander said. "She probably misses her friends."

"Maybe she should get together with Wordsworth."

*Yes!* I thought.

"Uh, I guess we could try it," Zander did not sound enthusiastic. "I'd just be nervous because your dog's so much bigger than Nicole."

"Wordsworth is the gentlest dog in the world," Dee Dee said. "He wouldn't hurt a fly."

"But you know how dogs can get a little wild when

y're playing," Zander said. "He might not mean to hurt her. He might just . . . you know . . . *sit* on her or something."

*Ow!* That really hurt my pride.

"Well, you decide," Dee Dee said. "If you want Nicole to play with Wordsworth, just bring her over after school some day."

"Okay, 'bye."

Dee started to push the baby carriage again.

*"Sit on her?"* I sputtered. "That's ridiculous!"

"Maybe you'll take losing weight more seriously now," Dee Dee said.


A little while later we got to Dr. Hopka's office. I hate to admit it, but I'd started whimpering with fear.

"If you really loved me, you wouldn't do this!" I cried.

"Be quiet," Dee Dee whispered. "We're here."

I heard a door creak open and the carriage bumped through. The air became heavy with the mixed scents of dogs, cats, and disinfectant. It was a smell that filled me with terror.

"What have we here?" a woman's voice asked, obviously puzzled by the baby carriage.

"Wordsworth Chandler, here for his annual checkup," Dee Dee announced.

"What's with the carriage?" asked the woman.

"Uh, he doesn't like long walks."

"That's a new one. Okay, let's take him in the back and weigh him."

Dee Dee pushed the carriage down a hall. Hands untied the blanket and I squinted up into the bright lights. An assistant wearing a white uniform stared down at me.

"Wow, he's big," she said.

"That's one of the reasons we're here," Dee Dee said.

"Can you help me get him out of the carriage?"

Dee Dee and the assistant reached in. Grunting and groaning, they managed to lift me out and put me on the large silver scale.

"Whew! He is one massive basset hound," the assistant said as she read the scale. "Eighty-seven pounds. Okay, take him in to the office and wait for the doctor."

The office had a table for me and a red plastic chair for Dee Dee. Against one wall were a white cabinet and a sink. From past visits I knew that the shots were kept in the cabinet. The assistant closed the door and left us in there. I crawled under the table and started to whimper again.

"Don't be scared." Dee Dee patted my head.

"That's easy for you to say," I grumbled.

"Even if he does give you a shot, it only hurts for a second."

"That's a second longer than I can stand!" I cried.

"I always thought dogs were brave."

"We are," I said. "But we also have very low thresholds of pain."

The door opened and Dr. Hopka came in. He's a short, fat, bald man with a sadistic smile. "Hello, Dee Dee," he said cheerfully. "How are you?"

I knew from experience that his cheerfulness simply masked the joy he got from torturing helpless animals.

"Fine, Dr. Hopka," Dee Dee answered.

"And how's Wordsworth?" Dr. Hopka bent down and looked under the table at me.

*Grrrrr!* I snarled and bared my teeth. I wasn't going down without a fight.

"Wordsworth!" Dee Dee gasped disapprovingly.

"Now, now." Dr. Hopka put on that fake gentle voice as he reached down for me. "I know this fellow. His bark has always been worse than his bite."

*Grrrrr!* Don't bet on it, Mac.

His hands went under my forelegs and he slowly pulled me out from under the table. Then he lifted me up. I should have bitten him, but I was afraid he'd drop me.

"My goodness!" Dr. Hopka groaned as he placed me on the table. "He has gotten large."

"Too large if you ask me," Dee Dee said.

I gave her a look that said, "No one asked *you.*"

Dr. Hopka poked me here and there, then placed his stethoscope against my heart. "Hmmm. That's an awfully fast heartbeat."

"I think he's worried about getting a shot," Dee Dee said.

"Oh, I don't know," Dr. Hopka said with a smile. "It's been a year since he was last here. It's hard to imagine he remembers."

"You'd be surprised," Dee Dee said.

I could picture that pointy silver needle. The memory of it piercing my fur made me light-headed.

Dr. Hopka felt along my spine and rib cage. "I'm afraid you're right, Dee Dee. Wordsworth has gotten much too heavy." He turned away toward the cabinet.

My heart started to pound even faster. I knew he was preparing the shot. The air in the room felt hot and stuffy. My breaths grew short and I started to feel dizzy. The last thing I remembered was hearing Dr. Hopka say something about a diet.

# Six

—∞∞∞—

**"I've been a veterinarian for twenty-five** years and this is the first time I ever saw a dog faint," someone said. "All I said was he had to go on a diet."

I opened my eyes. I was lying on my back. The room was spinning and I felt very woozy.

"Look, he opened his eyes!" That was Dee Dee's voice. Out of the blur I recognized her face, then Dr. Hopka's as he leaned over me.

"Are you all right, boy?" the vet asked, scratching my tummy.

*Groof!* I barked and rolled over. Of course I was all right. I wouldn't have fainted if the air in the examination room wasn't so stuffy. The *least* they could do was open a window.

"Looks like he's okay," Dr. Hopka said, putting his arms under me and lowering me to the ground. "Examination over."

Huh? What about the shot?

"But he fainted," Dee Dee said.

"I wouldn't worry about it unless he faints again," Dr. Hopka said.

"He doesn't have to get a shot?" Dee Dee asked as if she'd read my mind.

"I don't think so, but let me check." Dr. Hopka turned back to the cabinet and opened a folder.

Meanwhile, I glared angrily at Dee Dee. Gee, thanks for *reminding* him!

Dee Dee gave me a look in return, as if to say, "It's important."

I hoped I got to go along the next time *she* went to her doctor. I'd make sure to remind him of all the shots that would be good for *her*.

Dr. Hopka closed the folder. "Nope, he had the three-year rabies vaccine last year, so he doesn't get another one for two years."

"See?" Dee Dee said to me. "You had nothing to worry about."

Dee Dee often talks to me in front of others. Lots of people talk to their dogs. But I always have to remember not to answer.

"Well, that's not quite correct," Dr. Hopka said as he held open the examination room door for us. "Wordsworth has to worry about his weight, and you have to help him, Dee Dee."

"What should we do?" Dee Dee asked.

Dr. Hopka stopped at the front desk in the waiting

room and wrote something down on a piece of paper. "I want you to get him this special diet dog food. He should have two cups a day. One in the morning and one at night. And no more lamb chops or table scraps. And he must get more exercise. I'll be frank with you, Dee Dee, at the rate Wordsworth is going, he won't survive another two years unless he loses weight."

I was so happy about not having to get a shot that I'm not sure I was paying attention. Dr. Hopka handed the slip of paper to Dee Dee.

"Wordsworth's not going to like being on a diet," he said. "But in the long run, it's the best thing you can do."

Then he said good-bye and went into another examination room. Dee Dee kneeled down and clipped the leash to my collar. I went over to the baby carriage and nudged it with my head, then looked back at her.

"You can't be serious," Dee Dee said. "You need exercise, not rides in a baby carriage, Wordsworth."

"Is that his name, Wordsworth?" a woman sitting in the waiting room asked. "What a fabulous name."

Dee Dee and I both looked up. The woman had stylish black hair and was wearing a black jacket with gold buttons and black slacks.

"I'm Gladys Higgins," she said. "We're always looking for basset hounds and he's such a fabulous specimen. Maybe I should give you my card."

While she went into her purse for a card, Dee Dee asked what she wanted basset hounds for.

"I run a company called K–9 Incorporated," Ms. Higgins said. "We specialize in making gourmet dry dog foods."

She found a card and gave it to Dee Dee. "What's your name?"

"Dee Dee Chandler. What would you use Wordsworth for?"

"Why, in one of our commercials, of course," Ms. Higgins said.

"Really?"

"Well, I think he'd have to lose some weight first. But then he'd be fabulous, simply fabulous."

"You don't have to worry about him losing weight," Dee Dee said. "Dr. Hopka just put him on a diet."

"Good. Then I think there's a possibility we'll use him," Ms. Higgins said.

Dee Dee thanked her, then led me out of the office, pushing the empty baby carriage in front of her.

"This is my lucky day," I said when we were on the sidewalk outside. "First, no shot, and now maybe I'll get to be in a TV commercial."

"I think you have more important things to be concerned with," Dee Dee said.

"Like what?"

"Your diet."

# Seven

**She was right. It wasn't long before I** forgot all about Ms. Higgins and focused on only one thing: *food!*

"What a bummer," barked Charlie, the collie who lived across the street.

"Yeah, it shouldn't happen to a dog," added Madison, the brown Lab mix from around the corner.

Charlie and Madison were outside the fence around the Chandler's backyard. The leaves were falling and it was cold outside. I was inside the fence, practically dead from starvation. I'd just told them about the diet Dr. Hopka had put me on. I'd been on it for two days.

"Listen, guys, I'm really desperate," I groaned. "I can't stand that diet dog food. I have to get some table scraps or I'll die! Knock over a few garbage cans. I'll take anything you can find."

"I'll try," woofed Madison. "I'm always hungry, too. But

I have to warn you. Everyone's gotten wise lately. They're all using those cans with the tops that snap closed."

"Just try," I begged. "That's all I can ask."

"Okay, we'll see what we can do." Charlie and Madison went off to search for food. I lay down in the sun and listened to my stomach rumble.

About an hour later, someone scratched at the gate.

"Who is it?" I barked.

"Charlie and Madison," they barked back. "We found you something."

I jumped to my feet and hurried over to the gate just as they pushed something under it. It was long and whitish. A bone?

"What am I going to do with this?" I barked.

"It's a bone," woofed Madison.

"I can see what it is," I barked back.

"Well, you asked us to get you something and we did," barked Charlie.

"Jeez, guys, what am I gonna do with a bone?" I asked.

"Chew on it," Madison barked. "All dogs love bones."

"Not me," I barked. "I love *food*. This doesn't help at all."

"Wow, we searched the whole neighborhood and this is the thanks we get," grumbled Charlie.

"Yeah, you could at least show your appreciation," barked Madison.

"It's hard to show appreciation when you're starving to death," I growled.

• • •

"Wordsworth, you have to eat." Later that night, Dee Dee kneeled on the kitchen floor beside me and stroked my head. Not far away was my food bowl, filled with small brown pellets of something Dee Dee claimed was diet dog food.

"Wordsworth, please!" she begged.

My stomach grumbled and growled painfully. Water was the only thing I'd tasted since my visit to Dr. Hopka's office. I would have killed for a freshly broiled lamb chop.

"Talk to me," Dee Dee implored. "I'm worried about you."

"I'm worried about me, too," I said.

"You have to eat."

"If you want me to eat, give me something worth eating."

"I can't," Dee Dee replied. "You know I can't. Dr. Hopka says you have to go on a diet."

"Well, at least *he's* getting what he wants," I said.

"No, Wordsworth," Dee Dee said. "He doesn't want you to starve yourself to death. He just wants you to eat this diet dog food."

"It's horrible," I said.

"How do you know?" Dee Dee asked. "You haven't even tasted it."

"I can smell it. It smells like cardboard. If I wanted to eat cardboard, I'd eat a shoe box."

I guess Dee Dee decided to get tough with me because she said, "If you don't start eating, I'm going to have to call Dr. Hopka and tell him."

"So?"

"So maybe he'll give you a shot."

"I think you're making that up just to scare me into eating," I said.

"I'm serious, Wordsworth," she said. "If you don't eat, you'll get sick, and if you get sick, he may have to give you a shot."

"Ahem." Someone cleared their throat. Dee Dee and I looked up and saw Janine.

"Talking to that dog again?" Dee Dee's big sister asked with a smirk.

"So?" Dee Dee said, rising to her feet. "Lots of people talk to their dogs."

"That's true," Janine said. "But you're the only person I ever met who talked to their dog as if they expected the dog to answer."

"Maybe he will someday," Dee Dee said. "After all, he is very smart."

"If he's so smart, how come he hasn't eaten in two days?"

"Because he's smart enough to know that his new food tastes terrible."

I looked up in surprise. *Ah ha!* So even Dee Dee admitted it!

"It has to be better than starving to death," Janine said.

"That's what I've been telling him," Dee Dee said with a shrug. "But he won't listen."

"He won't listen because he's a dog, Dee Dee. He doesn't know what you're talking about."

"I think he does." Dee Dee crossed her arms resolutely.

Janine rolled her eyes and shook her head. "I can't believe someone as strange as you is my sister. Anyway, I came in here to show you what I just got."

She held up a magazine. On the cover was a photograph of a girl in a bathing suit. "My first catalogue."

"So?" Dee Dee said.

"So, now that I have a credit card, I can do my shopping at home," Janine said. "Why don't you take a break from that dog and help me pick out a new bathing suit?"

Janine sat down at the kitchen table. Dee Dee went over and sat down with her.

"Where'd you get it?" Dee Dee asked.

"My friend Muffy gave it to me." Janine started to thumb through the catalogue. "But now that I have my own credit card, I'll be getting lots of them in the mail. Muffy says she gets all kinds of catalogues."

"Wow, these are nice bathing suits," Dee Dee said.

"Yeah, and the prices are really good," said Janine.

"But this catalogue is from California," Dee Dee said. "You can't go all the way there just to buy a bathing suit."

"No, silly, I don't have to," said Janine. "All I have to do is call their toll-free number and place an order. They'll send the bathing suit here."

"But how do you pay them?" Dee Dee asked.

"I just told you. With this." Janine pulled a small silver card out of her pocket. "My new credit card. I just give them the credit card number and they send me the bathing suit."

"But then don't you have to pay the credit card company?" Dee Dee asked.

"Yes, at the end of the month," Janine said. "I'll give Mom and Dad my baby-sitting money, and they'll pay the credit card company for me."

"Cool," Dee Dee said. "So you can get this bathing suit now, and you don't even have to worry about paying for it until the end of the month."

"That's right." Janine smiled proudly.

"Do other people know about this?" Dee Dee asked.

"Dee Dee, the *whole world* knows about credit cards," Janine said. "The only reason you've never heard about them is because our parents are still living in the 1950s."

"Wow," Dee Dee said. "I can't wait until I'm a teenager and I can get a credit card."

# Eight

**The next morning was a Saturday and,** as usual in the Chandler house, everyone slept late. I woke up with a strange taste in my mouth. It tasted a little like cardboard. Stranger still, my food bowl was empty and my stomach wasn't growling as much.

"I don't believe it!" Dee Dee gasped a little later when she came down for breakfast.

"What, dear?" Flora asked from the kitchen table where she sat with her morning cup of coffee.

"Wordsworth ate his diet dog food."

No! It couldn't be! But that appeared to be the only logical explanation. My food bowl was empty and I only felt half as hungry as the day before. Still, I couldn't remember eating that horrible stuff.

Could I have eaten it in my sleep?

"Good boy, Wordsworth." Dee Dee patted me on the head.

Roy came in, rubbing his eyes and yawning. "Did anyone check the mail?"

"Not yet," said Leyland.

"Be right back." Roy hurried down the hall to the front door.

"Is he expecting something?" Flora asked.

"A letter from his girlfriend," Janine said with a yawn as she came into the kitchen.

Leyland looked surprised. "I didn't know Roy had a girlfriend."

"We're not sure he does," Janine said. "It depends on whether she writes back."

Roy returned to the kitchen looking glum and carrying a pile of magazines.

"No letter?" Flora asked.

Roy shook his head. "I've sent two more letters and still no reply. The only things that came were all these catalogues for Janine."

"Oh, cool!" Janine took them from him. She and Dee Dee quickly opened them and looked at all the things they offered for sale.

Flora looked concerned. "Now, remember, Janine, you have to pay for anything you order."

"I know," Janine said. "But it's still lots of fun to look. Oh, wow, here's one you'll like, Roy."

She passed him a catalogue filled with women in their underwear. Roy's face instantly turned red.

"Janine, please!" Flora gasped.

"Oh, come on, Mom," Janine said. "I just thought it would make Roy feel better about not getting a letter from Razel. Oh look, here's one for Wordsworth!"

Janine placed the catalogue on the floor. I got up slowly and strolled over in no great hurry. Just as I expected, the catalogue was filled with personalized dog collars, plastic dog toys, rawhide bones, and dog shampoo. Had I not been in the middle of a diet and semi-starved, I might have found it more interesting.

"Oops!" Janine grunted as some of the catalogues slid off the kitchen table and onto the floor.

One of them fell open right in front of me. I felt my eyes widen. This catalogue was filled with food! Golden brown meatloaves. Smoked turkey and hams! Oven-roasted prime rib with juicy red centers! Smoked pork and lamb! Steaks and cheeses! Mouth-watering cakes and pies! Candy apples and cookies and gingerbread! Cans of popcorn and pretzels!

*Owooooooooo!* A howl of uncontrollable yearning and despair burst from my throat.

Dee Dee reached down and took the catalogue away. "I don't think we should let Wordsworth see this one. It'll just remind him of all the things he can't have anymore."

Dee Dee added the food catalogue to the pile on the table.

Janine got up. "I guess I'll go upstairs and get dressed. We're all going to the city today, right?"

"Yes, dear," said Flora. "We're going to visit Great Aunt Emma and take her to a show."

"Boy, does that sound thrilling," Roy moped. "But I guess it's better than wasting another day waiting for a letter that'll probably never come."

They left the kitchen. As soon as they were gone, Flora turned to her husband.

"Leyland, darling," she said, "I'm worried about them."

"Janine and Roy?" Leyland's eyebrows rose curiously.

"Roy seems rather despondent about this young woman," Flora said.

Leyland nodded gravely. "Puppy love, darling. I'm afraid it's something we've all suffered through at one time or another."

"I suppose," Flora allowed with a sigh. "And I'm also worried about Janine and her credit card."

"Don't worry, dear," Leyland replied. "It's time for her to learn adult responsibilities."

It wasn't long before Leyland and Flora left the kitchen to get ready for their trip to the city.

"Come along, Dee Dee," Flora called. "Time to get ready."

"Just a minute," Dee Dee called back. As soon as she was alone with me, she kneeled down and patted me on the head. "I'm so proud of you, Wordsworth."

"Huh?" I was half asleep, lying on my side in a nice sunny spot near the sliding glass door.

"You finally ate your diet dog food," she said. "Dr. Hopka will be happy."

"I don't remember eating it," I said with a yawn.

"What?" Dee Dee looked puzzled.

I explained how I woke up with the taste of diet dog food in my mouth and something in my stomach. "I swear I don't remember eating it."

"You think you ate it in your sleep?" Dee Dee scowled.

"I guess so."

"Well, it doesn't matter as long as you ate it," she said.

Then she picked up my food bowl and went to the closet and put in another cup of those awful pellets. "And here's breakfast. I hope when I get back from the city later that you'll have fallen asleep and eaten it too."

"Don't bet on it," I grumbled.

Dee Dee kneeled down and petted me. "Wordsworth, do you really think I enjoy making you suffer like this? I know that dog food tastes horrible. I know you hate it. But you have to eat it. It's for your own good."

I knew she was right and I couldn't blame her. But there was no way I was going to eat any more of that diet dog food. At least, not while I was *awake!*

# Nine

**The Chandlers left for the city and I went** back to sleep. But it wasn't long before I woke up with a grumbling, hungry stomach again. If only there was something good to eat. I got up and sniffed around under the kitchen table for any tasty morsels that might have fallen off someone's plate at breakfast. Then I sniffed along the kitchen counters and checked the garbage can just in case someone had dropped something good in it.

But the pickings were sparse, and I knew I was about to face another hungry day. Losing weight and getting healthy was no fun at all.

I lay in the sun near the sliding glass door in the kitchen. As the day wore on, I was tortured by the memory of those wonderful meats, pies, and cookies in that catalogue I'd seen that morning.

When I napped I even dreamed about food. In my

**44**

dream a large truck pulled up in front of the Chandler's house and two men got out. They went around to the back of the truck and opened the big rear door. Other men began throwing down boxes to them. The men put the boxes on hand trucks. Then, grimacing under the weight, they wheeled all the boxes up to the Chandler's front porch.

Inside the boxes were those fabulous meats and cakes. I started to eat . . .

I couldn't stop . . .

I got bigger and fatter . . .

After a while I was as big as a house . . .

I made Clifford, the big red dog, look like a Pekinese!

I grew taller than the tallest tree. The ground beneath me started to give way under my weight!

I was sinking!

The earth was swallowing me up!

*Groooool!* I yelped in my sleep and woke up. My heart was beating wildly.

Okay, okay, I wouldn't eat quite that much.

I sat up. My stomach was growling more loudly than ever. I gazed longingly at the diet dog food in my bowl.

*No! No! Never!*

I needed to distract myself. I needed to remind myself of what good food really was. The more I thought about it, the more I wanted to see those fabulous pictures again. If I couldn't *eat* good food, at least I could *look* at it.

# Wordsworth and the Mail-Order Meatloaf Mess

The pile of catalogues was still on the kitchen table. Standing up on my hind legs with my front paws on one of the chairs, I managed to get my head partway over the table's edge and snap at the catalogues with my teeth. One by one, I pulled them down until the food catalogue fell to the floor.

Then very gently, with my paws and my nose, I peeled back the pages.

What a magnificent feast! But only for my eyes. My mouth watered as I looked at page after page of meats and other delicacies. Seeing them almost brought tears to my eyes. I had hoped that looking at the pictures would make me feel better, but instead, it only made me feel worse!

Roast duck! Pecan pie! Apple strudel!

*Meatloaf!*

I knew I should have stopped looking, but I couldn't. Page after page of fabulous foods . . . none of which I was allowed to have!

It wasn't fair. I'd always been a good dog, an obedient dog.

I didn't chew slippers.

I didn't bark noisily.

I wasn't supposed to suffer like this!

I wasn't supposed to starve.

If Janine could order things from catalogues, why couldn't I?

Hey! Wait a minute . . .

Maybe I could!

Grabbing the catalogue with my teeth, I headed for the stairs in the front hall. It had been a while since I'd climbed them. I used to climb them every night to sleep with Dee Dee, but recently I'd become content to sleep on my doggie bed in the kitchen.

But now I was a dog with a mission. I could only climb two or three steps at a time before I had to stop and rest. My tummy bumped against each step as I tried to get over it, but I knew that wasn't the real problem. The real problem was that I was weak from starvation. That's why I had to get some good food, some *real* food!

It was necessary for my survival!

Finally I got to Janine's room and collapsed on the floor. After resting a while, I dragged the catalogue over to her bed. Janine had her own phone, and like everything else in her room, it was on the floor. I tipped the receiver off with my nose and listened for the dial tone. There were lots of numbers in the food catalogue, but only one looked like a phone number. Again using my nose, I carefully pressed the buttons on the phone.

A ringing sound came from the receiver. I pressed my ear against it.

"Hello, this is the Fabulous Gourmet mail-order service, how may I help you?" a man's voice said.

"I'd like to order some meats," I said.

"Item number?" the man asked.

"Huh?" I didn't know what an item number was. "Sorry?"

"Next to each item is a number," the man on the phone explained. "That's how we identify what you want."

Uh-oh. There were lots of numbers. I wasn't sure which one he meant. Then I remembered something.

"Oh, dear, I've misplaced my reading glasses and I can't see a thing without them," I said.

"Can you at least tell me the page number?" the man asked.

I couldn't do that either. I had to think of something fast. On the page in front of me was that wonderful golden brown meatloaf.

"I want the meatloaf," I said.

"Oh, yes, the one on page eleven," he said. "It's one of our most popular items. Would you like the regular six-pound meatloaf or the extra-large twelve pounder?"

Recalling that awful dream, I decided not to make a pig of myself. "The six-pound loaf will be fine."

"Anything else?" the man asked.

There was lots more, but I didn't want to be greedy.

"And how would you like it shipped?" he asked.

"What are my choices?"

"Regular or overnight, which is ten dollars more."

Overnight meant I'd have a six-pound meatloaf the next day! I couldn't resist. "Overnight, please."

"Name on the credit card?" the man asked.

"Janine Chandler."

"Credit card number?" the man said.

*Credit card number?* Uh-oh. I didn't have that.

"Hello?" the man said. "I asked for your credit card number."

"I, uh, just realized I can't find it," I lied.

"Well, we can hold your order," the man said. "Just call us back when you find it."

"I will," I said with a heavy heart and an empty stomach. I had no choice but to nudge the receiver back onto the phone and hang up. My plan had failed.

# Ten

**Now that I was on the second floor, I** decided that I might as well stay. That was where Dee Dee found me that night when the Chandlers returned from the city.

"Wordsworth, what are you doing up here?" she asked.

I couldn't answer because the rest of the family had also come upstairs.

"I wonder if he missed us and came upstairs looking for us," Flora said.

Of course that wasn't the reason. Dee Dee knew it, but she decided to take advantage of the situation. She put her arms around my neck and hugged me. "Oh, Wordsworth, it's so sweet of you to come up. And since you're here, you can sleep in my room tonight."

"What a treat," Janine said, rolling her eyes sarcastically. Then she yawned. "I'm hitting the sack. I'm really wiped."

"Me, too," said Roy.

Soon everyone had gone to bed. I went into Dee Dee's room and lay down on the carpet. Dee Dee lay down on the floor so that we were nose to nose.

"Now tell me the truth," she whispered. "What *were* you doing up here?"

I obviously couldn't tell her the truth. Besides, I'd begun to concoct a new plan.

"I wanted to prove to you that I can go up and down the steps all by myself," I lied. "I thought it would be good exercise."

Dee Dee smiled. "I'm proud of you, Wordsworth."

"So we can stop this diet, right?"

Dee Dee shook her head. "Dr. Hopka wants you to stay on it until he sees you again."

"But don't I look thinner?" I asked. I must have looked thinner. I'd been *starving*!

Dee Dee raised her head and looked at me. "A little, but not enough to make a difference."

"Make a difference?" I gasped. "Do you want me to be all skin and bones?"

"No," Dee Dee said. "And that's why you have to keep eating your diet dog food. I noticed you didn't eat it today. I'm going downstairs to get it."

Before I could stop her, she'd gone downstairs and returned with my food bowl. She put it in the corner of her room. I wished she hadn't done that, because nothing in the world would make me eat that stuff. I'd rather starve.

# Wordsworth and the Mail-Order Meatloaf Mess

I slept in Dee Dee's room that night. I hadn't done that in a while. I was too large now to climb up on Dee Dee's bed, even with her help. So instead, Dee Dee got out her sleeping bag and laid it out next to me on the floor.

"Isn't this fun," she whispered in the dark, hugging my neck. "Just like old times."

"Hmmm." My stomach grumbled painfully.

"Oh, Wordsworth," Dee Dee said, stroking my snout. "I wish you were in a better mood."

"How can I be in a better mood when I'm starving to death?" I asked.

"Come on," she whispered. "It's not *that* bad."

"Easy for you to say," I said with a sniff. "You're not the one on the diet."

"Think of Nicole and how much more she'll like you when you're thinner."

"Every time I think of Nicole, she turns into a lamb chop."

"Oh, Wordsworth." Dee Dee let out an exasperated sigh. "I keep telling you this diet is for your own good."

"If it's for my own good, why does it feel so bad?"

Dee Dee kissed my head and hugged me. "I love you, Wordsworth, but sometimes you're impossible."

"Emaciated is more like it."

"That's enough," she said. "Now let's go to sleep."

●　　　　●　　　　●

I must have slept for a while. When I woke, I was no longer lying next to Dee Dee. In fact, I wasn't lying at all. I was standing. A strong scent of cardboard was in my nose. Looking down in the dark I was struck by a sickening realization. Right under my nose was my food bowl filled with those awful diet dog food pellets.

Oh no! I'd been sleep*eating* again!

I quickly backed away from the bowl, disgusted with myself. This was a new low. I came from a long line of distinguished basset hounds. My forefathers had been royalty! What would they say now if they knew I was eating diet dog food?

That was the last straw. I had to preserve my dignity. Now that Janine was home, her credit card must be around somewhere. I was going to find it and order that meatloaf if it was the last thing I did.

I crept quietly out of Dee Dee's room and down the hall to Janine's. Janine had her own bathroom, lit by a small night-light so she wouldn't bump into things in the dark.

I knew that what I was about to do was the act of a desperate dog, but I couldn't help myself. Quietly and carefully, I picked up Janine's phone in my mouth and carried it into the bathroom. Then I went back into her bedroom and found her jeans. Janine didn't carry a wallet or a bag. She always put her money, keys, and credit card in her pockets. Nudging with my paws and pulling with my teeth, I managed to turn the pocket inside out.

# Wordsworth and the Mail-Order Meatloaf Mess

Moments later, with the silver credit card in my mouth, I crept back into the bathroom.

I tipped the receiver off the phone and pressed redial. I could hear a ringing sound on the other end and then someone answered, "Fabulous Gourmet mail-order. How can I help you?"

Thank goodness for twenty-four-hour service.

"Hello," I whispered. "I placed an order this afternoon, but didn't have my credit card."

"Last name?"

"Chandler."

"Yup, here it is. You've got your credit card now?"

"Yes."

"Could you read the number to me?"

In the dim glow of the night-light, I read off the numbers.

"Will we be shipping to the same address as the credit card billing address?"

"Yes," I said.

"Thank you. Your order will go out tomorrow morning. You should have it the following day."

I knew what I'd done was wrong. But I was driven by instinct . . . by survival of the fittest. And if I didn't get that meatloaf soon, I was going to have a fit!

# Eleven

⚬⚬⚬

**Two mornings later I got up early and** sat by the front door. When Leyland went out to get the newspaper, I went out with him. The air was cold, the branches on the trees were bare. I sat on the porch and shivered. A little while later, Dee Dee came out in her bathrobe. She pressed her arms around herself. White vapor came out of her mouth when she talked.

"What are you doing out here, Wordsworth?"

Since the rest of the family was inside, I answered in a low voice. "Just wanted a breath of fresh morning air."

Dee Dee gave me a suspicious look. "You've never wanted that before."

"Well, I have to fill myself up with *something*," I pouted.

"Oh, poor Wordsworth." Dee Dee patted me on the head. "I know you hate me for doing this. But someday you'll thank me."

"Don't bet on it," I grumbled.

# Wordsworth and the Mail-Order Meatloaf Mess

A little while later, Dee Dee and Roy went off to school on their bicycles. A girl in a car stopped by and picked up Janine. Leyland left for the city to see his patent lawyer about a new invention, and Flora took the car to go to an art class.

I sat on the porch and waited. After a while, Madison came by with Cody, the yellow Lab who lived a few houses down the block. They came up to the porch steps and stopped.

"Hey, Wordsworth," Cody barked. "Heard they put you on a diet."

"Uh huh."

"My owners did that to me last year," Cody barked. "It wasn't so bad."

"Maybe not for you," I muttered.

"Listen, once you lose the weight, you'll be glad," Cody barked.

"Thanks," I grumbled.

"Hey, I'm just trying to be helpful," Cody barked. "You don't have to be such a grouch."

"I'm starving, okay?" I snapped.

"Jeez, let's get out of here," Cody woofed to Madison. "Wordsworth's no fun at all."

Cody started off, but Madison lagged behind. "Hey, uh, Wordsworth, I know this is like a touchy subject for you right now, but you're not the only hungry dog around. You wouldn't happen to know where I could get a quick snack, would you?"

I was just about to tell him to get lost when I suddenly thought of something.

"Matter of fact, I do," I barked.

Madison's ears perked up. "No kidding?"

"Go around to the backyard," I barked. "You know where the hole under the fence is?"

"Sure."

"Go through it, then up the deck stairs and through my doggie door into the kitchen," I barked. "There's a bowl of delicious gourmet diet dog food in there."

Madison hesitated. "You sure you don't want it?"

"Not this morning."

"Wow, thanks." Madison dashed around toward the back of the house.

A little while later he came back. "Thanks, Wordsworth."

"You ate it all?" I asked, amazed.

"A little more than half," Madison barked. "Stuff tasted like cardboard, but I was really hungry."

"Feel free to come back and eat more any time you want," I barked.

"Gee, Wordsworth, you're all heart," Madison barked sarcastically and left.

Around midmorning, the mail carrier passed the Chandler house but didn't stop. A little later, Roy rode up on his bicycle. It must have been lunchtime at school.

# Wordsworth and the Mail-Order Meatloaf Mess

"Hey, Wordsworth, mail come yet?" he asked as he climbed up the front steps.

*Groof!* I answered him like a dog.

Roy looked in the mailbox and frowned. "Darn!" He turned and trudged back down the porch steps with sagging shoulders. "I've written her eight letters and she hasn't written back once."

Ah, the poignant heartbreak of unrequited teenaged love. I felt bad for him.

On the other hand, maybe someday he'd have to go on a diet. Then he'd *really* know what heartbreak was like.

Roy got on his bike and rode back to school.

I waited on the porch.

And waited.

That mail-order meatloaf had to come. It just *had* too!

Around three in the afternoon, a red, white, and blue van pulled up to the house. A man in a blue uniform got out and took a box out of the back. Up on the porch, I stood and wagged my tail excitedly.

The man started toward the house. When he saw me he stopped and looked a little nervous. "You're friendly, right?"

*Grooof!* I barked happily and wagged my tail some more.

"Okay." He started up the porch steps. "I'm just gonna ring the bell and give this package to someone in the house."

What? He couldn't do that. He had to give *me* the package. That was *my* meatloaf!

*Grrrrrr!* I clenched my teeth and growled. My tail went down.

"Uh-oh." The delivery man stopped on the second step. "Guess you don't like that idea."

*Grrrrrr!* I growled again. He'd better believe it!

"Okay, okay," the delivery man said. He looked at the label on the box. "Hmmm. The company says this box contains perishable goods. It's not to be returned. They say that if for any reason the package cannot be accepted, I'm to leave it as close to the house as possible. So here you go."

He put the box down on the steps and hurried back to the van.

*Grooof!* I barked happily and started wagging my tail again. As soon as the van was out of sight, I grabbed the box in my jaws and headed for the backyard.

# Twelve

**It took me three days to finish that first** meatloaf. It was about the size of a loaf of bread and absolutely fantastic! Probably the best I'd ever had. I could have eaten the whole thing in one day, but I wanted to pace myself.

Until the next one arrived.

It took three days to eat that one too, and just as I finished it, the third arrived. This was great! All I had to do was call the Fabulous Gourmet mail-order service every three days and renew my order. I was in meatloaf heaven!

Dee Dee was right. I was thankful she'd put me on a diet. Otherwise, I never would have figured out how to mail order meatloaf!

"Boy, Wordsworth sure seems to be in a good mood lately," Janine said at dinner one night.

"Yes," said Flora. "I've noticed that he doesn't beg for scraps at the table anymore."

# Wordsworth and the Mail-Order Meatloaf Mess

"That's because he's learned that we're not going to give him any," said Dee Dee.

The other members of the family gave each other doubtful looks.

"I don't know, Dee Dee," said Janine. "Wordsworth's pretty persistent when he wants something. It's not like him to just give up."

*Briinnng!* The kitchen phone started to ring. As usual, everyone looked at Janine.

"Why are you all looking at me?" she asked. "If it was for me, they'd call my phone upstairs."

"The boys still call you on this phone around dinnertime because they know you'll be down here," Dee Dee reminded her.

"Well, sometimes," Janine admitted.

*Briinnng!*

"I'll get it," Roy said, jumping up.

"He's hoping it's Razel," Janine whispered.

"Hello?" Roy answered eagerly. Then his face fell. "Oh, uh, just a minute." He put his hand over the phone. "It's some lady calling about dog food."

Leyland frowned and shook his head. "Tell her we're in the middle of dinner and we're not interested."

"Sorry, we're not interested," Roy said and hung up. Then he trudged back to the table.

Flora looked concerned. "Roy, darling, why the long face?"

Roy shrugged and didn't answer.

**63**

"He was hoping it was Razel," Janine said.

"Was not!" Roy snapped.

"Touchy, touchy." Janine teased him.

"Stop it," Flora said. "That's not very nice, Janine. You shouldn't make fun of Roy's feelings."

She was right. I went over and put my head in Roy's lap, just to let him know someone cared.

Roy patted my head. "Thanks, Wordsworth."

Out of the corner of my eye, I saw Dee Dee staring at me with a skeptical look on her face.

"Oh, by the way," Leyland said. "Your mother and I have decided we're taking the family to visit Uncle Steve and Aunt Brenda for Thanksgiving."

"But they live in Boston," Roy said.

"That's right," said Leyland. "We'll fly up the night before Thanksgiving."

"When will we come back?" Dee Dee asked.

"We can stay all weekend if you like," said Flora.

"Cool!" For the first time in weeks, Roy actually smiled.

"No, it's not," Janine said. "I have a field hockey tournament the day after Thanksgiving. I really don't want to miss it."

Leyland and Flora exchanged a look.

"We understand, darling," Flora said. "In that case we'll fly back first thing Friday morning. That way you'll be home in time for your tournament."

"Thanks, Mom."

"What about Wordsworth?" Dee Dee asked.

"I'm sorry, sweetheart, but we can't take him on an airplane," Leyland said.

"Yeah, he's probably over the weight limit," Janine quipped.

"That's not funny," Dee Dee shot back. "We've never left him alone before. Who's going to walk him?"

"He can go out through the doggie door whenever he wants," Flora said.

"What about food?" Dee Dee asked. "Who's going to feed him?"

The question of food was a good one. Thanks to Madison's daily visits to my food bowl, Dee Dee actually believed that I was eating that disgusting diet dog food.

"Ah, I have just the answer!" Leyland rose to his feet. "Stay here. I'll be right back."

Leyland hurried down the hall and went through the basement door.

Janine winked at Roy. "A drumroll please."

Roy started to drum his fingers against the kitchen table.

"Ladies and gentlemen!" Janine announced. "It is time for another . . . Leyland Chandler invention!"

A moment later Leyland returned with something about the size of the kitchen garbage can. It had a slot at the bottom and a small digital clock on top.

Janine pretended to be shocked. "A time bomb, Dad? Don't tell me . . . we're not going to leave Wordsworth here and blow him up!"

"It's not funny." Dee Dee crossed her arms and pouted.

"Have a sense of humor," Janine said.

"It's the Chandler Automatic Dry Dog Food Dispenser," Leyland announced with pride. "Here's how it works. You put in several days' worth of dog food. Then you set the frequency of feeding. For Wordsworth, that would be twice a day. Then you set the time of feeding, let's say eight in the morning and eight at night. Then you set the amount to be fed at each feeding, so that would be a cup. And voila!"

He pressed a button and a cup's worth of diet dog food appeared through the slot at the bottom of the machine.

"Good invention," Janine said.

"Bravo!" Flora clapped.

"Dad, this one actually has marketing potential," Roy said.

"I don't like it," Dee Dee said.

"Why not?" asked her father.

"Because it means leaving Wordsworth alone. He's part of our family and he should go everywhere we go."

"Give me a break, Dee Dee," Janine said. "He's just a dog."

Dee Dee looked like she might burst into tears.

"No, I think Dee Dee's right," Leyland said. "This invention isn't necessarily for us, although I would like to try it while we're in Boston. But remember, Dee Dee, there are many people who, for whatever reason, might find the Chandler Automatic Dry Dog Food Dispenser, uh . . . *indispensable* at some time in their lives."

"Some pun, Dad," Roy groaned.

"But what if something goes wrong and Wordsworth doesn't get his food?" Dee Dee asked.

"It's a very simple device and I've tested it numerous times," Leyland said. "But even if it were to fail, Wordsworth would only miss a few meals."

"Don't worry, Dee Dee, he'll be fine," Janine said. She got up and brought her dishes to the sink. The rest of the family did the same.

"Whose turn is it to do the dishes?" Flora asked.

"Mine," Dee Dee said with an unhappy shrug.

Dee Dee's parents and older sister left the room. Dee Dee slowly pulled on the yellow rubber gloves and ran hot water into the sink. Roy stayed behind and brought his plate toward her.

"Hey, come on, Dee Dee," he said softly. "It's not that bad."

"I just hate leaving Wordsworth," Dee Dee said with a sniff. "What if something happens?"

"Wordsworth is a pretty smart dog," Roy said.

I sure hoped Dee Dee didn't argue with *that.*

"I know," she said. "But I'll miss him."

Roy put his hand on her shoulder. I'd never seen him do that before. "Yeah, you probably will. Just like I miss Razel. At least we'll get to do our missing together."

Dee Dee smiled slightly. "Thanks, Roy."

Roy left the kitchen. As soon as he was gone, Dee Dee turned to me. "What do you think?"

"I think love has changed Roy," I said.

"I know. I guess it's cute. But I meant, about us going away and leaving you alone."

"Oh . . ." To me that meant the freedom to eat meatloaf without worrying about being caught. "It's okay. I understand."

Dee Dee gave me a suspicious look. "Roy's not the only one who's changed around here. So have you."

"Me?" I said, acting surprised. "I'm the same old loveable basset hound I've always been."

Dee Dee gave me that look again.

"You don't believe me?" I asked.

"I don't know what to believe," Dee Dee said. "All I know is when you first went on this diet you turned into an irritable, unfriendly dog. Now suddenly you're friendly again."

"I guess it just took me some time to get used to it," I said.

Dee Dee studied me closely. "The strange thing is, you don't look like you've lost any more weight."

# Thirteen

———— ❦❦❦ ————

**The mail-order meatloaves kept coming.**
I kept eating them. Life was good. I was a happy dog.

Each time a meatloaf came, I would drag it into the backyard and tear the box open. Then I would take out the meatloaf and dig a hole in the ground to hide the box. By the time I finished covering the box with dirt, I'd developed a nice healthy appetite.

Every morning after the kids went to school, Madison came in through the doggie door and ate the diet dog food.

One morning I watched him wolf down that vile stuff and lick his chops.

"Don't they feed you at home?" I asked.

"Oh, sure," Madison barked. "They feed me fine. But I'm a growing dog. I could eat all day and not gain weight."

"Yes, you would," I barked.

"Nope." Madison shook his head. "My vet says it's because I have a very fast metabolism."

**69**

"A what?" I asked.

"A fast metabolism," Madison barked. "See, your metabolism is the process by which your body uses energy from the food you eat. I have a very fast metabolism so I can eat a lot of food and my body just burns it up. Like I'll probably go out now and run around the park for a couple of hours."

"You will?" I asked in disbelief.

"Oh, sure. I do that almost every day. If I lay around the house all the time like you, I'd go nuts."

"Will you always have a fast metabolism?" I asked jealously. I would have given *anything* for a fast metabolism. Just imagine being able to eat *all day and not gain weight!* That was my idea of heaven!

"Naw, as you get older, your metabolism slows down," Madison barked. "That's what happened with you, Wordsworth. Remember when you were a puppy and you ran around all the time?"

I shook my head. Even as a puppy I never ran.

"Well, you know what other puppies are like," Madison barked. "As you get older, your metabolism slows down. You don't run around as much and you don't need as much to eat."

It was starting to make sense.

"Thanks for explaining that to me," I barked. "Now you better scoot before Flora comes in."

"See you tomorrow." Madison crawled through the doggie door and left.

# Wordsworth and the Mail-Order Meatloaf Mess

· · ·

It turned out to be a sunny, warm afternoon. A new meatloaf arrived, and I took it out to the backyard and unwrapped it. Then I settled down for a feast. After a while, I heard dog voices coming from the other side of the fence.

"You smell that?"

"Yeah, it smells great!"

"I could smell it all the way over on Circle Drive."

"Where do you think it's coming from?"

"I hate to say it, but over there. From the other side of the fence."

"You mean, Wordsworth's backyard?"

"Bummer!"

"Yeah, he never shares anything."

Oooch! That hurt. By now I recognized the voices. They were from Charlie, Fluffy, and Cody, dogs I considered my friends. I looked down at my brand-new meatloaf. Then I looked over at the fence.

"Guys?" I barked. "That you?"

"Yeah, Wordsworth," Fluffy barked back. "Smells pretty good. Enjoying yourself?"

It wasn't easy to say what I said next, but I did it. "Want some?"

"You mean it?" Charlie barked.

"Sure, guys," I barked. "You're my friends. Come through the hole."

In a flash they crawled through the hole under the fence. I broke off large chunks of meatloaf to give to each of them.

"Wow, Wordsworth, this is great!" Fluffy barked. "Where'd you get it?"

"Uh, from a friend," I barked.

"Well, thanks a lot for sharing it!" barked Cody.

"You're a good guy, Wordsworth," Charlie barked. "I take back all the mean things I ever said about you."

"Hey, listen, guys," I barked. "Come back tomorrow. There'll be more."

"Great!" "Thanks!" "What a guy!"

As soon as they left, I went back into the house to order another meatloaf. Now that I was sharing it with my friends, I figured I might want to move up to the larger twelve-pound size.

I had just finished ordering it when Roy came through the front door looking gloomy. In his hand were a couple of envelopes.

"Another day and no letter from Razel," he moaned when he saw me. "Just bills. Hmmm, looks like Janine got her first credit card bill."

*Credit card bill?* I suddenly stopped. Uh-oh, that meant trouble.

As usual, Roy left the mail on the small table by the front door. I waited until he went upstairs, then I hurried over to the table. Getting up on my hind legs, I managed to sweep the letters onto the floor.

# Wordsworth and the Mail-Order Meatloaf Mess

But which one was Janine's credit card bill? I got down and sniffed them, hoping one would smell like Janine's credit card. None did, but one did have a design that resembled the design on the credit card. I took a chance and tore it open. Yup, there were those long columns of numbers.

Of course, I couldn't let Janine see the bill. If I did, she'd want to know who ordered all those meatloaves. It would take Dee Dee about a millisecond to figure out what was going on, and then I'd be sunk.

The answer to this problem was obvious. I picked up the bill in my mouth and went out my doggie door to the backyard. There I dug a hole and buried it.

By then I was pretty tired from all the activity. It was still warm out, so I decided to lie down on the grass and take a nap.

Once again, I had that dream where I kept eating and eating and growing and growing until the ground beneath me began to collapse and I started to sink into the earth.

"Wordsworth!" Someone was shaking my shoulder. "Wordsworth, wake up!"

I opened my eyes. It was dark out. I was lying on the lawn, panting. My heart was beating like a drum. Dee Dee was kneeling over me.

"Are you okay?" she whispered.

"Uh, yeah, sure." I rolled over onto my feet. Even in the dark I could see that Dee Dee looked worried.

"You sure?" she asked. "You were twisting around and yelping. I thought you were having a heart attack."

"Just a bad dream," I whispered back.

"About what?"

"Uh, that's strange. I forgot."

Dee Dee gave me an odd look.

"Really," I said. "I forgot."

"It's not that," she said. "I just don't understand why you don't look any thinner. I know you're eating that diet dog food. Are your friends smuggling scraps to you?"

"No, honest."

"I just don't get it."

"It's probably my metabolism," I said.

"Your what?" Dee Dee gave me a funny look.

"My metabolism," I said. Then I explained all about food intake and energy. When I finished, Dee Dee was still looking at me funny.

"How do you know about that?" she asked.

"I've been talking to my friends."

"About your *metabolisms?*" Dee Dee asked skeptically.

"Just because they're dogs doesn't mean they're not well educated," I said.

"If you say so." Dee Dee turned and went back up the deck stairs, shaking her head.

# Fourteen

———⚋⚋⚋———

**From that day on, I ordered an extra-**
large meatloaf every other day and shared it with my
friends. I even developed a good relationship with the
overnight delivery man. Every other afternoon I'd wait
on the porch for his van to arrive. He'd get out with my
package and start up the stairs. That's when I'd growl.
Then he'd put the package down and leave.

Soon all my friends in the neighborhood were coming by each afternoon to join me in a feast. The extra-
large twelve-pound meatloaf was the size of a really
large loaf of bread. That meant there was plenty.

"Hey, what's going on?" a dog barked one afternoon
while Charlie, Fluffy, and I ate.

"Who's that?" I asked.

"Madison, I think," barked Charlie.

"Come under the fence," I barked.

Madison came under the fence, and I gave him a
piece of meatloaf. He quickly ate it.

**75**

"Where'd you get this, Wordsworth?" he asked.

"He been getting them for weeks," Fluffy barked happily. "We come over every afternoon and have a feast."

Madison's jaw dropped. "I can't believe it!" he gasped. "These guys have been eating gourmet meatloaf while I got stuck with that lousy diet dog food?"

"Listen, if you don't eat that stuff, this whole scheme is over," I barked. "I have to keep my family thinking I'm eating diet dog food."

"Well, okay," Madison barked. "But I should get a piece of meatloaf every day, too, just like Charlie and Fluffy."

"Okay," I barked. "It's a deal."

"Hey, smells good!" another dog barked from the other side of the fence.

I recognized the voice and barked back, "Come on over, Cody."

"Can I bring a friend?" she barked.

"Sure, why not?" I barked back. "There's plenty to go around."

A moment later Cody came through the hole under the fence with her "friend." I couldn't believe my eyes! It was Nicole!

"Wordsworth, this is Nicole," Cody barked. "She's new around here."

"Uh, hi, Nicole, nice to meet you again," I barked. My heart started to pound.

"Hi, Wordsworth," Nicole barked demurely.

Cody's eyes widened. "You two have met before?"

I said that we had.

"Well, in *that* case, I'll leave you alone." Cody smiled and helped herself to some meatloaf.

I grinned at Nicole, hoping I didn't look as nervous as I felt. "So, I never did ask you where you were from."

"Pretty far away," Nicole barked. "We had to drive in the car for two days to get here."

"Are your owners nice?" I asked.

"Very nice," Nicole barked. "But they don't give me meatloaf every day. You must have really great owners to give you enough meatloaf for you *and* your friends."

"Yeah, well, they're very special people, and they realize how valuable I am to them," I barked proudly.

"Why?" Nicole asked innocently.

"Well, for one thing, they say I'm an exceptional guard dog," I barked. "A few months ago I not only trapped two burglars in a tree, but I aided in their capture as well."

"How brave!" Nicole gasped.

"Later, the same two burglars kidnapped me and held me for ransom," I barked. "But I managed to escape. I also helped rescue a damsel in distress whose sailboat was sinking in a storm."

Nicole's pretty brown eyes widened. I could see that she was very impressed.

"My hero," someone sighed.

I turned around to see that it was Cody. The other dogs were all smirking.

"Hey, it's true," I barked.

"You're just man's best friend," barked Charlie with a wink.

"But Wordsworth's owners must think very highly of him to give him such good food," Nicole barked.

"I'll tell you a little secret," I barked, moving closer to her. "My owners do whatever I tell them."

"Now *that's* a good one," Cody barked with a chuckle.

"It's true," I barked.

"Prove it," barked Madison.

"Okay, I will," I barked. "You know how all our owners are going to have big Thanksgiving feasts next week?"

"Sure," barked Cody. "But they always put me outside so I won't get into anything."

"Yeah," barked Charlie. "*They* get to eat well, but for us it's just another dog day."

"Well, this year that's all going to change," I barked. "We're going to have a big Thanksgiving feast right here in honor of Nicole. We'll have only the finest meats and pies for everyone who comes. How's that?"

Charlie shook his head.

"What's wrong?" I asked.

"Look, Wordsworth," he barked. "I don't know how you've managed to get these meatloaves, but there's no way you can throw a party like that. You're a dog, not a human."

"Yeah," cracked Cody. "They're not gonna let you go shopping at the Grand Union, you know."

The other dogs chuckled.

"Just wait and see," I replied confidently.

My friends gave each other quizzical looks. I knew they were wondering if I could really do it.

"But you don't have to have a party for me," Nicole barked.

"I don't *have* to, but I *want* to," I barked.

"But why?"

"Let's just say it would be a small token of my esteem," I barked with a wink.

"Really?" Nicole gasped.

"Hey, it's the least I could do," I barked with a smile.

"That's so nice!" Nicole cried.

I thought for a moment she was going to kiss me. Then a human voice called, "Here, Nicole! Hey, Nicole, where are you?"

"Oh, that's Zander," Nicole barked, looking back toward the fence. "I guess I have to go. You don't really have to give me a party, Wordsworth."

"But I insist," I barked. "Let's have it next Thursday. Right here. Same time, same place."

Nicole gave me a dreamy look. "Okay," she barked. "Thursday. See you then."

"Looking forward to it," I barked back.

"And thanks for the meatloaf," she called.

She went through the hole under the fence and we

heard Zander say, "So there you are, Nicole. I couldn't figure out what happened to you."

Meanwhile, in my backyard, Madison finished eating his meatloaf and yawned. "A big feast, huh, Wordsworth? Sounds pretty good."

"Well, I'll believe it when I see it," Cody barked.

"He better come up with something," Charlie barked. "Or Nicole is going to be very disappointed."

"Don't worry, guys," I barked. "I've got it all under control."

# Fifteen

**"I just don't understand it, Dr. Hopka,"**
Dee Dee was saying. "The only thing Wordsworth eats
is the diet dog food."

We were back at his office for my one-month follow-
up visit.

"That's the only thing you *see* him eating," Dr.
Hopka replied, giving me a knowing look. "Believe me,
Dee Dee, he's eating a lot more than that. According to
the scale, Wordsworth now weighs eighty-nine pounds.
He's the first dog I've ever seen go on a diet and *gain*
weight."

"But couldn't it just be that his metabolism has
changed?" Dee Dee asked.

"Metabolisms do change, Dee Dee," Dr. Hopka said.
"But it takes years, not weeks. All I can tell you is that
he's getting food from somewhere, and it behooves you
to find out from where and make sure it stops."

# Wordsworth and the Mail-Order Meatloaf Mess

Dee Dee gave me an angry, frustrated look. I knew I was going to have some explaining to do once we got back outside.

Dr. Hopka put his face in front of mine. "I get the feeling you're a pretty smart dog, Wordsworth. But if you were really smart, you'd know that gaining all this weight is very bad for you. You better wise up before it's too late."

A little while later, outside the office, Dee Dee silently clipped the leash on my collar. This time I'd walked to Dr. Hopka's under my own power. It seemed silly to make Dee Dee push me in the baby carriage, and I didn't want to risk running into Nicole and Zander again.

We started walking home and Dee Dee gave me an angry look. "I'm mad at you, Wordsworth. Where have you been getting food from?"

I couldn't lie to her. "From a friend."

Dee Dee nodded. "Then I'm very disappointed in you. You said you weren't getting scraps from anyone and you lied. Do you really want to have a heart attack?"

"No."

"Well, then you better stop accepting food from friends and get back on your diet," Dee Dee warned.

Deep in my heart, I knew she and Dr. Hopka were right. I would have to stop eating meatloaf every day. Right then and there I made a decision. I would stop . . . just as soon as the Thanksgiving feast for Nicole was over.

• • •

We arrived back at the Chandlers' just in time for dinner.

The Chandlers, as always, fended for themselves. They each made their own meal. But then they sat down and ate together.

"You know what's weird?" asked Janine, who, as usual, had brought home a sub from the sub shop in town. "I've had my credit card for over a month, and I still haven't gotten a bill."

"Sometimes the first bill takes longer because you're new to the system," said Leyland, who was having a bowl of split pea soup.

"I wouldn't complain," said Roy, who was munching on a triple-decker peanut-butter-and-jelly sandwich. "That just means that you have extra time before you have to pay."

"I know," said Janine. "I just hope that something isn't wrong."

I felt a little funny about that, since I knew something *was* wrong. Two bills had come from Janine's credit card company, but I'd buried them both in the backyard.

"Well, I know one thing that's wrong," Dee Dee said. "I took Wordsworth to Dr. Hopka's today for his follow-up visit. And instead of losing weight, he's actually gained two pounds."

"How is that possible, dear?" Flora asked.

"That's what I want to know," Dee Dee said. "I think he's been getting food from his friends. Has anyone here been feeding him?"

The other members of the family shook their heads and went on eating.

After dinner the family was going to the movies. The Chandlers were all great fans of movies and frequently went to them. While they were getting ready to go, Dee Dee decided to take me for a walk.

I gave her the saddest look possible. After all, I'd already walked all the way to Dr. Hopka's and back that day.

"Don't look at me like that," Dee Dee warned. "Dr. Hopka said you need lots of exercise. Another short walk won't hurt."

Dee Dee went to get the leash, and I went outside ahead of her, using the doggie door. As I went through it, I noticed that my sides rubbed against the sides of the opening. That was odd, but I didn't think much of it.

Dee Dee joined me outside and we started down Magnolia Drive.

"I'm really disappointed in you, Wordsworth," Dee Dee said. "I've tried so hard to get you healthy and you've been dishonest."

I winced. When she put it that way, it really hurt. I hadn't *meant* to do anything dishonest. I simply liked to eat.

"From now on I expect you to start slimming down,"

she said. "I want you to promise me you won't accept any more food from friends."

"I promise," I said. After all, the Fabulous Gourmet mail-order service wasn't my friend. It was just a catalogue.

Up ahead I saw Madison coming toward us, being walked by his owner.

"Hi, Wordsworth," Madison barked. "Got any more of that delicious meatloaf?"

"Not today," I barked back. "But you can still come and eat my diet dog food."

"Naw, forget it," Madison barked. "I'll wait for the meatloaf."

"You can't do that!" I barked. "If that diet dog food isn't gone, Dee Dee's gonna get suspicious, and that'll be the end of the meatloaf."

"Well, how come I'm the only one who has to eat it?" Madison barked. "When do Charlie, Cody, and Fluffy get a turn?"

"Look," I barked. "I don't care who eats that stuff as long as *someone* does. If you can get one of the others to come over tonight, that's fine. Get a stranger for all I care. Just make sure it happens."

"That's a deal!" Madison barked.

"What was all that about?" Dee Dee asked when we started walking again.

"Oh, nothing," I said.

Dee Dee gave me a suspicious look. "Seemed like an

awful lot of barking for it to be about nothing. Are you up to something, Wordsworth?"

"No!" I gasped. "Of course not. He, er, was just telling me about a new dog bed he got."

"What about it?"

"Uh . . . " I had to think of something fast. "It's a water bed."

"A water bed for dogs?" Dee Dee frowned.

"Well, that's what's so interesting," I said. "You know how Madison's part Lab, and Labs love to swim? Well, it's made just for dogs that like to swim."

"Oh." Dee Dee still looked puzzled. Worse, I started to feel really bad about lying to her. In a way, I was starting to wish I hadn't ordered those meatloaves because now I had to lie all the time. I promised myself I'd stop soon . . . just as soon as my Thanksgiving feast was finished.

Dee Dee took me back home. Then she and the others left for the movie. A little while later, Charlie appeared on the back deck.

"Madison said I had to come over," he barked. "Something about dog food."

I explained the situation to him. He didn't look happy.

"I can't come in and eat it," he barked. "I can't fit through your doggie door."

He was right. Charlie was a collie and too tall to fit through. I was even having trouble getting through it.

"Wait there," I barked. Then I went over to the food

bowl and pushed it to the doggie door. "Just stick your head in."

Charlie stuck his head through the doggie door and took a bite. "Yuck! This stuff tastes like cardboard!"

"I know, but someone has to eat it," I barked.

"Oh, okay," Charlie grumbled and took another bite. "So how's the party coming?"

"Fine," I barked. I planned to order everything as soon as Charlie left.

"I can't believe your owners are going to do this for you," Charlie barked. "What else are you getting besides meatloaf?"

"I thought I'd get some cold cuts and a smoked turkey," I barked. "After all, it is Thanksgiving."

"How about party favors?"

I hadn't thought of that, but why not?

"I bet you're getting something really nice for Nicole," Charlie barked with a wink.

Hmmm . . . Charlie was full of good ideas.

A little while later, he finished the diet dog food.

"Whew, I hope Madison finds someone else to eat that stuff next," he barked. "See you at the party!"

"You bet," I barked back.

Charlie went back down the deck steps and through the hole under the fence. Now it was time to order for the party. I was worried about putting more charges on Janine's credit card. Since this was the last time I was ever going to order anything over the phone, I decided that it would be better to charge the stuff to someone else in the family. Take Roy for instance. I didn't think Roy had a credit card so I decided to make one up for him. I promised myself I'd use it just this once and never again.

I called the Fabulous Gourmet and gave them my last order ever. Since it would be for the party, I decided I might want some variety, so I ordered a sliced roast beef and a smoked ham in addition to two large meatloaves and a turkey. I had it all sent to Roy and made up a charge number for him.

Then, remembering what Charlie had said, I called the dog accessory catalogue and ordered lots of squeaky toys, beef jerky, rawhide bones, and a beautiful collar with Nicole's name embroidered on it.

I had just hung up Janine's phone when I heard the door open downstairs. The Chandlers were back! Oh-oh! I couldn't let them find me upstairs! I scooted out of the room and into the upstairs hallway.

"Wordsworth?" Dee Dee yelled downstairs. "Wordsworth, where are you?"

I started to bump down the stairs. Whoa! I lost my balance!

*Thump-a-Thump-a-Thump!* The next thing I knew, I was falling, rolling, and bouncing down the stairs!

*Ow! Ooch! Yeowch! . . . Thunk!*

I hit the floor at the bottom of the steps and lay on my side panting. Everyone except Dee Dee was standing there looking down at me in shock. I heard footsteps as Dee Dee rushed in from the kitchen.

"Oh my gosh!" She quickly kneeled down and put her arms around my neck. "Wordsworth, are you all right?"

I just groaned. I couldn't talk because the rest of the family was standing there.

"Did you see that?" Roy asked. "Wordsworth fell all the way down the stairs."

"Do you think there's something wrong with him?" Flora asked.

"Yeah, I think he's so fat he can't handle his own momentum," Janine said.

"That's mean," Dee Dee snapped. "At least he's trying to lose weight."

"How hard can he be trying if he keeps gaining instead of losing?" Janine asked.

"Just leave him alone," Dee Dee said angrily.

The rest of the family left. Dee Dee sat next to me, rubbing my head. "Don't let them hurt your feelings, Wordsworth. I just looked in your food bowl. All your diet dog food is gone. I'm proud of you, Wordsworth. You've finally decided to lose weight."

Soon, I thought. Soon.

# Sixteen

**"She wrote! She wrote back!" The sounds** of Roy's shouts woke me the day before Thanksgiving. I could tell by the position of the sun in the sky that I'd slept late.

"Guess what, everybody?" Roy stood at the bottom of the stairs and shouted up gleefully. "Razel wrote back!"

The rest of the family came downstairs in their pajamas and robes. Obviously, they'd slept late too.

"Wow, I can't believe she wrote back after all this time," Janine said.

"What's it say?" Dee Dee asked eagerly.

"Yeah, tell us, Roy," said Janine. "Did she seal it with a kiss?"

"Now, now," said Flora. "This is Roy's private correspondence. He doesn't have to share it with us if he doesn't want to."

"It's okay," Roy said, looking down at the letter. "It says, 'Dear Roy, Thank you for all your letters. I'm sorry I didn't write back sooner, but I've been super busy with school. I just wanted you to know that I'll be coming up to Soundview Manor to visit the Kavanaughs on the day after Thanksgiving. I hope you'll be around. See you then. Best wishes, Razel.'"

Roy looked up with a big grin. "She's coming the day after tomorrow!"

"That's wonderful news," Flora said happily.

"There wasn't any other mail, was there?" Janine asked.

"Just this." Roy handed her a letter. "It's from your credit card company."

"Must be the bill," Janine said. "It's about time."

Uh-oh, I thought nervously.

"I can't believe how long it took for them to send me this," Janine said, tearing the letter open. She started to read it and her jaw dropped. "Oh no!"

"What's wrong?" Dee Dee asked.

"They're canceling my credit card for nonpayment!" Janine gasped. "They're turning over my account to a collection agency!"

"How can that be?" Flora asked. "This is the first bill they've ever sent you."

"They say they've tried repeatedly," Janine said. "And listen to this! They say I owe them almost a thousand dollars! That's impossible! All I bought was a bathing suit!"

"Does it say what was bought with all that money?" Flora asked.

"Things from a place called *Fabulous Gourmet*," Janine said.

That's when I glanced up and noticed that Dee Dee was giving me another funny look. I looked away.

"Well, it doesn't really matter," said Leyland. "An error has clearly been made."

"I'll say," said Janine. "And I'm going to call them right now."

"No, darling, it will have to wait," Leyland said. "We've slept too late. If we don't get dressed and leave right now, we're going to miss our plane to Boston. Whatever the problem is, it will wait until we get back."

"But—" Janine started to say.

"Your father's right," said Flora. "We mustn't miss our plane. You'll have to take care of it when you get back."

"Now come on, everyone, let's get dressed," Leyland said.

Everyone except Dee Dee went back upstairs. She stayed and gave me another look.

"Why do I get the feeling that Janine's credit card problem has something to do with you not losing weight?" she asked.

"I don't know," I said innocently.

"Dee Dee!" Flora called from upstairs. "You must come up and get dressed at once!"

**94**

"Coming!" Dee Dee yelled back, and turned to me. "We're going to talk about this when I get back, Wordsworth." Then she headed up the stairs.

A little while later the family came down dressed and ready to go.

"Oops, almost forgot the Chandler Automatic Dry Dog Food Dispenser!" Leyland hurried into the kitchen to fill it with diet dog food.

A few moments later he returned and pulled open the front door. Everyone except Dee Dee went out.

"Come on, Dee Dee," Roy yelled from the front steps.

"Coming," Dee Dee yelled back. Then she turned and studied me. "Tell me the truth, Wordsworth," she said in a low voice. "Do you know anything about it?"

"About what?" I asked.

"About why they canceled Janine's credit card."

I shook my head, but I couldn't look Dee Dee in the eye.

"Come on, Dee Dee," Roy yelled again. "We have to leave!"

"Be good, Wordsworth." Dee Dee kissed me on the top of the head. "We'll be back the day after tomorrow."

Dee Dee pulled the door closed. I had a feeling I was going to be in big trouble when she got back. But all I could think about just then was the party.

# Seventeen

~~~~~~~

**It took me quite a while that night to** move all the food and party favors from under the front porch, around to the back of the house, through the hole under the fence, and into the backyard. Then I had to dig holes and bury all the boxes. It was tiring work, and by the time I finished, I was very tired and very, very hungry.

I was just about to go back into the house when I realized there was nothing to eat. After all that work I knew I wouldn't get to sleep without a snack, so I took one of the giant-size meatloaves with me. I wasn't going to eat the whole thing. I just wanted a little snack. I always slept better on a full stomach.

# Eighteen

**The sound of scratching at the kitchen** window woke me the next morning. I opened my eyes and saw Cody waiting on the deck.

I tried to get up, but I felt sluggish and bloated.

"Is it your turn?" I asked.

Cody nodded.

"Come on in," I barked.

Cody came in. I managed to get on my feet, but it was a real struggle. The memory of the night before came back to me. I'd brought in one of those extra-large meatloaves. But there'd been plenty left over. Where could it have gone?

Cody gave me a funny look.

"What's wrong?" I asked.

"I hate to say this, Wordsworth, but you don't look too good this morning," she barked.

I didn't feel too good either. In fact, I felt like I'd

swallowed a bowling ball. The skin around my tummy felt like it was stretched so tight it might burst.

Cody started to eat the diet dog food in Leyland's automatic dry dog food dispenser.

Meanwhile, I looked around the kitchen, for the rest of the meatloaf, but it was nowhere in sight. What could have happened to it? And why did I feel so bloated this morning?

"Wow, that's the worst stuff I ever tasted," Cody groaned after she finished the diet dog food.

"Well, I'll make it up to you at the party," I barked.

"So when's it going to start?" she asked, licking her chops.

"We can start right now," I barked. "Why don't you go tell everybody. And don't forget Nicole, okay?"

"Sure thing." Cody went through the doggie door, down the steps, across the backyard, and through the hole under the fence. Then she started barking, telling all our friends about the party.

A little while later all my friends were in the backyard, eating meatloaf and roast beef and smoked turkey. They were playing with the squeaky toys and chewing happily on the rawhide bones. Nicole was there, along with Cody, Charlie, Madison, Fluffy, and all the rest. The only dog missing was me. I was still in the kitchen, waiting to make a grand entrance and give Nicole the special gift I'd ordered for her.

# Wordsworth and the Mail-Order Meatloaf Mess

"Hey, Wordsworth!" Charlie barked. "Aren't you going to come out and join the party?"

"Yeah, Wordsworth," barked Cody. "This is your bash. You have to be part of it."

The rest of the dogs turned and began to bark at me to come out. They came up the deck stairs and gathered in front of my doggie door.

It was time for my grand entrance. Wordsworth, the greatest party-throwing dog in history, was about to make his appearance.

I picked up the special personalized dog collar I'd ordered for Nicole and stepped toward the doggie door.

I put my head through.

And then my right front paw.

Then my left front paw.

And then . . . I stopped.

I was stuck. The rest of me wouldn't fit through the doggie door!

How is this possible?

I tried to squeeze through the doggie door. Suddenly, a burp rose out of my stomach. Hmmm . . . tasted like . . . meatloaf! The realization of what must have happened hit me like a ton of dog biscuits. I'd eaten it in my sleep! The whole extra-large meatloaf! That's why I'd felt so sluggish and bloated this morning! That's why I couldn't fit through the doggie door!

This had to be the most embarrassing thing that had

ever happened to me. Thinking fast, I put the personalized collar down on the deck.

"Nicole, this is a special gift for you," I barked, "to show how delighted I am that you've come to Soundview Manor."

"Oh, Wordsworth!" Nicole gasped. "You shouldn't have."

"You're a beautiful canine," I barked. "And you deserve a beautiful collar."

Nicole smiled. Then she moved close and kissed me.

All my friends howled and barked happily.

"Go on, everyone!" I shouted. "Keep partying!"

"All right!" "Yahoo!" "Let's boogie!" The dogs all tramped back down the deck steps and into the backyard and started playing again.

Only Nicole remained behind, smiling at me. "Thank you, Wordsworth. It's the nicest thing anyone's ever given me."

"You deserve it," I barked with a smile. "Now, go on and enjoy yourself. This party is in your honor."

"Aren't you going to join us?" Nicole asked.

"I'd like to, but I'm afraid I can't," I barked, scrambling for an excuse. "You see, I, er, I absolutely promised my owners that I would guard the house for them and wouldn't leave it under any circumstances. So I have to stay inside."

"But surely you could come out to the backyard," Nicole barked.

I shook my head. "A promise is a promise. I told them I'd stay in the house."

Nicole just sighed and gave me a dreamy look. "You really are an exceptional guard dog. I'll always remember you, Wordsworth."

"You can do better than remember me," I barked. "Why don't we get together again next week?"

I hoped that by then I wouldn't be stuck in the doggie door anymore.

"Oh, I'd love to, Wordsworth, but we're all going back home tomorrow," Nicole barked.

"Home? I thought you lived here."

"Oh, no. We've just been visiting," Nicole barked. "But I'll always remember you and Soundview Manor. You've made my stay here really nice."

Then she picked up her new collar and went down the steps and joined the party. *She was leaving tomorrow?* I lay down and closed my eyes. What a fiasco!

# Nineteen

———— ⪘ ————

**The party lasted until dark. By then my** friends had finished all the food. They took their toys and beef jerky party favors, thanked me, and left. Only one dog didn't get to enjoy the party—me.

I stayed jammed in the doggie door. I'd managed to wedge myself in so tightly that I couldn't go forward and I couldn't back up.

That's where Dee Dee found me the next morning when she and her family returned from Boston.

She was the first one into the kitchen. "Wordsworth, what are you doing in the doggie door?" she whispered.

"I'm stuck!" I whispered back.

"How long have you been like this?"

"All night."

Now the rest of the family came in.

"What the devil?" Leyland said.

"He's stuck," Dee Dee said.

"How?"

"I don't know," Dee Dee said, "but I guess it's pretty obvious that he hasn't lost any weight."

With Leyland and Roy pushing from the outside, and Dee Dee and Janine pulling from the inside, they managed to get me out of the doggie door and back into the kitchen.

"I don't know what Wordsworth's been eating," Roy said, "but it sure hasn't been diet dog food."

He pointed at Leyland's automatic dog food dispenser. A day's worth of dog pellets overflowed from the bowl. Dee Dee gave me a stern look. I had a feeling I was about to get the lecture of my life.

Then the doorbell rang.

"That must be Razel!" Roy cried and dashed down the hall.

He opened the front door, but Razel wasn't there. Two men wearing dark blue windbreakers were.

"Uh, can I help you?" Roy asked.

Both men held open wallets that displayed gold badges and identification cards. "We're from the Federal Bureau of Investigation."

"The FBI?" Roy's eyes widened. By now the rest of the family had joined him at the door.

"Is one of you Roy Chandler?" one of the agents asked.

"Uh, I am," Roy said.

"You're under arrest," the agent said.

The Chandlers watched in amazement as the FBI agent turned Roy around and handcuffed his hands behind him.

"What'd I do?" Roy gasped.

"You are charged with violating United States Penal Code, Title 23, Section 648, credit card fraud," the FBI man said. "You are hereby warned that anything you say may be used as evidence against you in a court of law. You have the right to remain silent and have legal representation. If you cannot afford private representation, you will be provided with court appointed legal counsel."

"Excuse me, but I think there's been a mistake," Leyland said. "Roy's only fourteen years old. He doesn't even have a credit card."

The men in the blue windbreakers leveled their gazes at Leyland. "I'm sorry," one of them said, "but the FBI does not make mistakes."

The next thing we knew, the FBI led Roy down the front steps toward a dark sedan.

# Twenty

———⟨⟩———

**"Wait a minute!"** Leyland said and ran down the steps. "This clearly must be a mistake, and I can prove it with one phone call."

The FBI men stopped and frowned. "How?"

"Please come into the house and I'll show you," Leyland said.

Leyland led them back into the house and to the kitchen where he picked up the phone and dialed.

Meanwhile, Janine, Dee Dee, and I stayed by the front door. Once again, I noticed Dee Dee giving me a funny look, as if she suspected I knew something.

"Wordsworth," she said. "I think it's time you and I took a walk."

"How can you take Wordsworth for a walk at a time like this?" Janine asked. "Your brother has just been arrested. We have to find out what's going on."

"I bet we'll know a lot more once I've taken Wordsworth for a walk," Dee Dee replied and went to get my leash. She brought it back and was just putting it on me when the doorbell rang again.

"Now what?" Janine asked, pulling open the door. Outside stood Razel.

"Hi, guys," she said. "Is Roy around?"

"Yes," said Dee Dee, "but the FBI just came and arrested him."

Razel looked shocked.

"Nice move, Dee Dee," Janine groaned. "Why don't you come in, Razel. It must be some kind of a mistake."

Janine led Razel toward the kitchen. I started to follow, but then I felt my leash go tight. I turned and looked back at Dee Dee.

"Not so fast," she said, opening the front door. "You're coming with me."

# Twenty-one

**Dee Dee and I took a long walk. I had to** tell her the truth. I couldn't lie anymore. I was ashamed of myself. Janine was in debt for nearly $1,000 and Roy had just been arrested by the FBI . . . all because I couldn't control my appetite.

"I don't know what we're going to do," Dee Dee said sadly. "But we'll have to do *something*."

Dee Dee and I stayed out for hours. Not only because we took a long walk, but because I'd gotten so fat that I couldn't go more than few dozen yards without pausing to rest and catch my breath.

When we got home, a small red sports car was parked in the driveway.

"What are you going to tell your parents?" I asked.

"I guess I'll have to tell them the truth, Wordsworth," Dee Dee said. "I mean, I really love you and would never want anything bad to happen, but we can't let Roy be arrested when it's your fault."

"But then they'll arrest me," I said. "I'll be the first dog ever arrested for credit card fraud. I'll become the most infamous dog ever. Dogs everywhere will hate me."

"We have to do what's right," Dee Dee said as we went up the front steps. "You have to be brave, Wordsworth. You have to accept your punishment like a man."

"But I'm not a man, I'm a dog."

The front door opened. Roy came out carrying ice skates.

"Hey, Dee Dee," He said cheerfully, "where have you been?"

"We took a walk," Dee Dee said in shock. "What happened with the FBI?"

"Oh, Dad took care of it," Roy said. "I'd explain it, but I just told Razel I'd meet her to go ice skating. See ya."

Roy hurried down the steps and started to jog down the sidewalk. Dee Dee tugged on my leash. "Come on, Wordsworth, we have to find out what happened."

We rushed into the house. Just as we got in the door, Janine came down the stairs in her field hockey uniform.

"You're going to your tournament?" Dee Dee asked in wonder.

"Of course," Janine said. "I'd never miss it."

"But what about that huge credit card bill?"

"Oh, Dad took care of that," Janine said as she got her jacket out of the closet. "See you later."

The next thing we knew, she pulled open the front door and went out. Dee Dee looked at me in wonder. "Now we *really* have to find out what's going on!" she whispered.

Just then a woman's voice came from the kitchen. "Oh, it's simply fabulous, Mr. Chandler. Absolutely fabulous!"

Dee Dee and I gave each other a funny look. Somehow, we'd heard that voice before.

We went into the kitchen. Leyland was standing there . . . with Gladys Higgins, the dog food lady we'd met at Dr. Hopka's. She bent down and patted me on the head.

"Wordsworth, you fabulous basset hound, what are you doing here?" she asked.

"We live here," Dee Dee said.

"You do?" Ms. Higgins looked surprised. "What a fabulous coincidence!"

"Excuse me, Dad," Dee Dee said. "What happened to Roy? I just saw him."

"The FBI had to let him go," Leyland said.

"Why?"

"Well, it turned out that almost every order went to some place called the Fabulous Gourmet," he said. "I called them up and asked if they ever tape-recorded their telephone orders. They said that they always did. Then I insisted that the FBI listen to the tapes of the orders Roy allegedly made. They listened and the voice making the orders was much deeper and obviously different than

Roy's. It became clear that someone else did the ordering and then intercepted the goods before they got to our house. After all, they didn't find a shred of evidence in the house."

Dee Dee and I shared an amazed look.

"And what about Janine?" Dee Dee asked.

"Same thing," Leyland said. "Someone else ordered with her credit card and then intercepted the goods. I simply demonstrated that the overnight delivery company didn't have a single signature from anyone in our family showing that we accepted a package. Not only did the FBI drop all its charges against Roy, but the credit card company is issuing Janine a brand-new credit card."

"But someone still owes the credit card company almost a thousand dollars," Dee Dee said, glancing at me.

"Yes, and whoever that person is, I hope they get caught and are made to pay," Leyland said.

"Then all of Roy's and Janine's problems are over?" Dee Dee asked in amazement.

"Yes," Leyland said. "And not only that, but Ms. Higgins here has decided to buy the manufacturing rights to the Chandler Automatic Dry Dog Food Dispenser."

"Aren't you the lady we met at Dr. Hopka's office?" Dee Dee asked.

"That's correct, Dee Dee," Ms. Higgins said. "And I'm so delighted to run into you again because K-9 Incorporated has just launched a brand-new dog food product, and I think Wordsworth will be perfect for it."

"Well, that's really nice, but as you can see, the last thing we want Wordsworth to do right now is eat more food," Dee Dee said.

"But that's why he'll be perfect," Ms. Higgins said. "You see, we've decided to get into the gourmet diet dog food business. There's a tremendous demand. Only one other company makes a diet dog food and, quite frankly, theirs tastes like cardboard. On the other hand, our new product, Low-Cal Canine Kibblets, tastes simply fabulous! What we'd like to do is a before and after program with Wordsworth, taking pictures of him every two weeks as he loses the weight. We'll pay you a thousand dollars for agreeing."

I saw a sparkle in Dee Dee's eye. A thousand dollars was just what we needed to pay back the credit card company for all the meatloaves I'd ordered.

"I think you've got yourself a deal!" Dee Dee said, shaking Ms. Higgins's hand. Then she turned to me. "Am I right, Wordsworth?"

I gave her a weak smile. It wasn't like I had much choice.

"You know what?" Ms. Higgins said, opening her bag. "I just happen to have a sample with me. Perhaps Wordsworth would like to try some."

"I'm sure he would," Dee Dee said. "After all, it's something he's going to have to get used to very quickly."

Ms. Higgins kneeled down and held out her hand. In it were half a dozen small pellets.

# Wordsworth and the Mail-Order Meatloaf Mess

I sniffed them. They didn't smell like cardboard. They smelled much more like . . . tissue paper!

I backed away a little and gave Dee Dee a pleading look.

She crossed her arms and narrowed her eyes.

I knew I wasn't going to get out of this. I licked my chops and pretended to be hungry. It was time to bite the Kibblet.

**Todd Strasser** has written many award-wining novels for young and teenage readers. He speaks frequently at schools about the craft of writing and conducts writing workshops for young people. He lives with his wife, children, and dog in a place near the water.

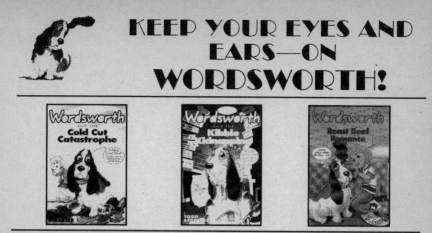

# KEEP YOUR EYES AND EARS—ON WORDSWORTH!

Wordsworth is a very smart talking Basset Hound and a member of a very strange family, the Chandlers. There's the utterly inept Mrs. Chandler, the bumbling Mr. Chandler, sixteen-year-old Janine—a pretty jock who'd rather play sports than date boys, fourteen-year-old uncoordinated Roy who would do just about *anything* for a date, and ten-year-old Dee Dee, wise beyond her years, who, together with clever Wordsworth, tries to keep the rest of the family out of trouble!

# IT'S WORDSWORTH AND THE . . .
## COLD CUT CATASTROPHE
## KIBBLE KIDNAPPING
## ROAST BEEF ROMANCE
## MAIL-ORDER MEATLOAF MESS
## TASTY TREAT TRICK* *coming soon

Visa & Mastercard holders—for fastest service call 1-800-331-3761

MAIL TO: HarperCollins*Publishers*
P.O. Box 588 Dunmore, PA 18512-0588

**Yes! Please send me the books I have checked:**
❑ **COLD CUT CATASTROPHE** 106257-X . . . . . .$2.99 U.S./$3.99 CAN.
❑ **KIBBLE KIDNAPPING** 106258-8 . . . . . . . . . .$2.99 U.S./$3.99 CAN.
❑ **ROAST BEEF ROMANCE** 106288-X . . . . . .$2.99 U.S./$3.99 CAN.
❑ **MAIL-ORDER MEATLOAF MESS** 106326-6 . .$3.50 U.S./$4.50 CAN.
❑ **TASTY TREAT TRICK** 106327-4 . . . . . . . . . .$3.50 U.S./$4.50 CAN.

SUBTOTAL . . . . . . . . . . . . . . . . . . . . . . . . . . . .$_____
POSTAGE AND HANDLING . . . . . . . . . . . . . . . . . . . . . .$_____ 2.00
SALES TAX (Add applicable sales tax) . . . . . . . . . . .$_____
TOTAL . . . . . . . . . . . . . . . . . . . . . . . . . . . . . .$_____
Name_____
Address_____
City_____ State_____Zip_____

Remit in U.S. funds. Do not send cash. (Valid only in U.S. & Canada.) Allow up to 6 weeks for delivery.
Prices subject to change.                                    H10611